ACROSS THE GREAT RIVER

IRENE BELTRAN HERNANDEZ

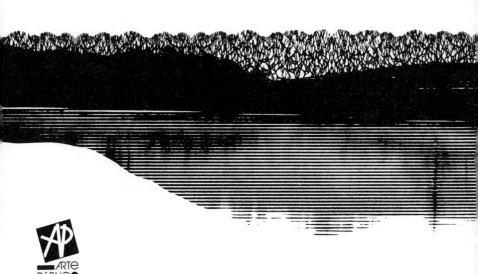

AP
ARTE
PÚBLICO
PRESS

This volume is made possible by a grant from the National Endowment for the Arts, a federal agency, and the Texas Commission for the Arts.

Recovering the past, creating the future.

Arte Público Press
University of Houston
Houston, Texas 77204-2090

Hernández, Irene Beltrán, 1945–
    Across the great river / by Irene Beltrán Hernández
    p. cm.
    ISBN 0-934770-96-4
    I. Title
    PS3558.E6873A65
    813'54—dc19   89-289
                                                                        CIP

The paper used in this publication meets the minimum requirements of the American National Standard for Permanence of Paper for Printed Library Materials Z39.48-1984. ⊚

Across the Great River

Irene Beltrán Hernández

Chapter One

I watch Mama tie a leather pouch around her waist. She slips a black skirt over it, then turns to fetch her sandals. She bends to tie them on, then moves to the table. She puts bread and a piece of dried meat in a scarf, then she ties the ends of the scarf together into one tight knot. Now, she waits.

"Where are we going, Mama?" I ask.

"On a trip, Kata. Now, dress quickly."

"But Mama, it's still dark outside."

She looks at me sadly. "Kata, I wish we weren't going anywhere, but . . ."

Papa enters the hut. For a moment they stare at each other, but I cannot tell if they are angry. He moves to his cot and picks up his guitar which he slings carefully over his shoulder. "Have you got the pouch?" he asks.

Mama touches her waist. "Yes, but Carlos, it is such a long walk for the children." She picks up Pablito, my baby brother, and hugs him tightly. I watch as she dries her tears on the baby's shirt. With red eyes she looks around our hut, then she comes over and touches my shoulder. "M'ija, daughter, is there something you would like to take on this trip?"

"Will we be gone long?" I ask.

Again she sobs, then turns her back to me. I hear her blow her nose as I walk over to my cot. I reach under my serape and pull out my cloth doll. "Can I take Anna?"

"Yes, now come. Papa is waiting for us outside." She hands me the scarf. I hurry out the door after her.

The night air wakens me as I follow them. This is strange, I think. Why are we going for a walk in the middle of the night? Papa trudges ahead like a soldier going to battle. He takes such giant steps that it is hard for us to keep up with him. Mama takes two steps for each one of Papa's and I take four and still I fall behind.

Mama runs to catch him. "Carlos, we are leaving the only home we know. In the name of all that is good, please change your mind and let us return to our warm hut." She clings to his arm, but still he walks onward.

"We cannot return! This is a dream that I shall make come true." He walks onward removing himself from her grip.

"Carlos! Some dreams are not meant to be! This dream of yours is wild and very dangerous!" she cries.

"Silence! I will hear no more!" he commands as he walks on even faster.

Mama stops walking and stares at Papa's back. I grab onto her skirt. "Mama, don't cry. See, the stars aren't sad." She hugs me tightly, then takes my bundle. I am glad because the bundle is getting heavy. Besides, I have Anna to carry. I run to catch up with Papa. He is such a tall man, so thin and so brown. I take his free hand and kiss it. He smiles down at me, showing white teeth under a thick mustache.

I glance around. This path is in the middle of nothing but empty land. A tree sprouts up here and there on the desert, and the moonlight is flooding the land as the sun does in the daytime. I keep walking, switching Anna from hand to hand.

"M'ija, daughter, get away from the brush. You might trip on a cactus or uncover a rattler. Stay behind me."

I obey Papa instantly. "Are we going to the river, Papa?" He does not answer, but moves as if he were turning the world under his feet. Walking on, I find myself thirsty. "I want a drink, Papa."

"Soon, daughter, soon," he says, but he does not stop walking.

I look back at Mama, who seems to have slowed down. Her long skirt hugs her thin legs. She puts the scarf with the food on top of her head and balances it. She is small but strong, and her thick black hair is braided in a massive pigtail which swings back and forth with each step she takes. Her face glows in the moonlight, reflecting a quiet sadness.

"We will stop here to wait." Papa points to a spot covered with high brush. Mama sits on a nearby rock and I flop down next to her. Papa then hands her Pablito.

As I rest, I notice they seem frightened. Papa's pacing back and forth worries me. Mama is cradling Pablito. How I envy Pablito, sound asleep like a fat lazy cat on a Sunday afternoon.

"Quiet! We must not make a sound!" warns Papa.

Mama sobs, "Carlos, there is still time for us to turn back. Our family is here in Mexico."

"Woman, I have made up my mind." Papa takes his hat off and rubs his brow, then paces back and forth a few times. "I will return shortly. Remember, stay here and do not move. Do you understand, Kata?"

"Yes, Papa." I touch Mama's calloused hand. Her palm is sweaty. A stray lock of her hair falls forward. She nervously pushes it back in place. Then she bends to kiss Pablito and breaks into heavy sobs. She raises her tear-stained face, then pulls me closer to her side.

I look up into her face. She kisses my forehead, then bends her head in prayer. From between her breasts she pulls out her beads. Mama never goes anywhere without them. Fifty-nine beads in all. Each one represents a prayer.

I wonder how Mama remembers all those prayers. She says them nightly.

The night becomes silent. I can no longer hear Papa's footsteps and I can hear Mama's breathing, but not my own. I put my hand to my chest. My heart is pounding away, and I wonder why. Suddenly, a branch breaks. Mama stiffens. I hear him returning, too. Papa is like a big shadow that comes from behind the clouds. "Come," he says, "they are waiting." He takes Pablito from Mama's arms.

"Carlos, I am afraid." Mama mutters.

He turns and faces her, then he gently brushes her hair back. "Do not fear, my love. All is ready and a new life across the border awaits us." He bends and kisses her forehead, then squeezes her shoulder. "Come, we do this for the children's sake."

She takes my hand and picks up the bundle. Then, she bites her lips and rushes along as if she wishes to punish me. We walk downhill. Papa stops. From behind a tree appears another shadow.

"Señor," says the shadow. "We will accept your money, now." Papa turns back to Mama, who lifts her skirt and unties the pouch. I watch as Papa takes the pouch over to where the man stands and pours the entire contents onto the sand.

The shadow bends on his knees next to Papa. I listen while Papa counts the paper money out loud, then hands it to the man whose arm is eagerly out-stretched. The moonlight shines upon a large tattoo that is imprinted on the man's right arm. I walk over to his arm and take a closer look. It is the picture of a woman with some kind of rope around her waist. No, I decide. It is not a rope. The woman holds a snake in her hand. The snake's body is curled around her waist. I step away from the man at once. "Ah!" says the shadow. "What is this shiny stone that winks at me from within the sand?" I look to where he points, and there, within the sand, I see a golden yellow glow that seems to be a stone of some kind. Papa hurriedly takes the stone and some other coins and puts them back into the pouch. Then, he rises and straightens the guitar upon his back. "Let's get on with this, man!" demands Papa sternly.

The shadow rises, too. He has large teeth that sparkle white in the moonlight. "When you hear the call of the doves, proceed downhill to the river bank." Then, the shadow disappears into the high brush much like a cloud that is hidden within a dark sky.

Papa and I walk back to Mama. She says, "Carlos, I did not like that strange man."

"Nor did I, but it is too late. The money is gone and we must go on." He takes Pablito from her. We hear the cry of the doves and Papa moves ahead at a fast pace.

It is downhill all the way. We run, dodging rocks and cactus. In the moonlight, I can see that Pablito is no longer asleep. He bobs up and down on Papa's shoulder, crying in discomfort. Papa hushes Pablito, but the guitar strings play by themselves.

Papa and Pablito are way ahead of us. My legs spin as fast as a weaver's wheel. Without warning my feet go out from under me and I fall, causing Mama to lose her balance. She falls and we both roll and roll as a wheel rolls downhill. Then, she pushes me aside in one big thrust. "Carlos!" she screams. She stops abruptly against a cactus plant and screams as the thorns tear into the soft flesh of her arm. I sit up stunned with the taste of sand caked on my tongue.

Papa reaches us in one giant stride. He stands me up and checks my arms and legs. Then, he hands me the baby. He rushes back to Mama and stares down at the wound. He quickly examines her arm, then looks up to search the path. "Beloved, we shall remove the thorns later. Now, we must hurry because your screams might have alarmed them."

Mama nods that she understands and shakes the tears from her face. Papa takes Pablito and clutches my arm. We are off, running downhill like the wind.

I glance back at Mama who follows. Her arm must feel like burning fire, but still she is able to keep up with us. I see a visible cloud of dust rising rapidly behind her.

"Where are the clouds!" Papa snaps as if he is angry with them.

Papa's grip is like an iron bracelet choking my wrist. I want to tell him to let go, but I dare not, for I can see that he is very angry. Instead, I hold tightly to Anna.

Again, I hear the cry of the doves as it echoes out from the darkness. We run faster and soon strange voices become louder. The high weeds snap at my face an darms and the mud covers my feet. We approach the river bank where Papa stops. Still carrying Pablito, he wades out waist-deep to a boat where a man sits waiting. Papa hands him Pablito, then dashes back for me.

Papa carries me into the water, which feels cold against my legs. He loses his footing and we go under. The cold water surrounds me and chokes me. I hold tightly to Papa and to Anna and when we finally come up, I gasp. Papa lifts me onto the boat, then he turns to help Mama, who now waits on the river bank.

In the distance, I hear a motor as if a truck is

coming our way full speed. I glance up, and there on top of the hill I see two lights that zig-zag downhill. Then, I hear voices that echo four or five times. They say, "Alto! Stop! We will shoot!"

I hear a loud cracking pop, which seems to come from out of the heavens. Mama screams and I turn to see her fall into the water with a big splash. Mama and Papa go under, leaving nothing but circles of water floating everywhere.

Suddenly, two large lights beam upon the water. The man that sits in the boat moves quickly and shoves us down into the bottom of his raft. Pablito starts crying, and with his hand, the man signals me to quiet him. I hug Pablito, hoping to warm him, but my dress is wet and he pulls away. I hear whizzing sounds all around us. It sounds as though God has sent bolts of lightning to strike us, but soon they stop.

I peep into the water around me, searching for Mama and Papa. Then, I glance up at the huge man in the boat. He crouches low, letting the boat drift, rocking itself back and forth. Suddenly, they pop up beside us, and Papa shoves Mama into the boat.

"Go! Man, go quickly!" Papa yells.

The man shakes his head. "No, it's too far for you to swim. Come with us."

Small splashes of water again sprinkle around us and the whizzing noises start again. "Go! I will swim!" Papa demands before he goes under.

The boat lurches forward. I look to see that the river is now carrying Papa further away, but our boat moves in the opposite direction with greater speed. Soon, I cannot see Papa at all.

Once in a while a moan escapes from Mama's lips and she stirs. I look up at the big man with the gleaming eyes. He is sweating and the muscles on his arm jump as he rows. As the time passes, I grow tired of searching for Papa and I sigh, feeling very lost without him. I glance down at Pablito, who is sleeping against my arm. I wish I were he. He doesn't worry. He just sleeps and eats.

The man stops rowing and sits. Soon the rocking of the boat hushes me into drowsiness, but I force myself to stay awake as the boat glides through the water like a floating log. It soon stops against some tall brush sticking out of the water, and there we wait.

After some time, a voice from the river bank breaks the silence that surrounds us. "Chente," it says, "it is clear now."

The man in the boat pulls out the oars and rows, guiding the craft through high brush which gives way to land. He pulls in the oars and says, "Compadre, we had trouble this time. The woman is hurt and the children are wet and cold. Their man went under, trying to swim the river."

"Rotten luck!" answers the man on the bank who emerges from the shadows of a tree. He catches the rope that is thrown to him, then pulls in the boat and ties the rope around the tree. The man called Chente jumps out of the boat into the water. It comes to his waist. He turns and holds out his arms for the baby. "Pass him to me so that I may take him ashore."

I give him Pablito and he wades ashore and hands him to the other man. Then, he returns for me. He is strong and lifts me easily, then he carries me to the shore.

Mama moans loudly as he picks her up in his arms. It seems that they will fall into the cold water, but the man holds fast. When he reaches the bank of the river, he gently lays her on the ground. "She's in bad condition. We must get her to Doña Anita's right away." He lifts his head from Mama's chest. "Are you children, okay?" he asks.

I nod yes.

"Bueno. Good. We must be on our way to get help for your mother." He lifts Mama into his arms and motions for me to follow with Pablito. When I do not, he turns back. "Come!" he commands.

I cross my arms and stand frozen. "Papa is still out there!" I shout as I point back to the river we have just crossed.

"My friend will wait for your Papa. We must get help for your mother or she will die." He hurries up the steep path, and I follow him carrying Pablito. I catch him on top of the hill and I ask, "Where are we?"

He keeps walking, but answers, "No longer in Mexico, niña." His breathing is heavy. "You are in the land of good opportunity."

"But, what does that mean?" I ask, very puzzled.

He chuckles, "You are in the United States of America. The river we just crossed is called the Rio Grande. You are now in Texas."

"Is that good?" I ask, still curious.

"Si, yes. It is very good. You shall see."

Chapter Two

We make our way to the other side of the hill where a truck is parked. The bed of the truck is filled with hay, on which he lays Mama, and then he puts Pablito beside her. I climb in by myself.

"The ride will be bumpy because I must drive fast. You must hold tight or else you will fall out," he instructs. He goes to the front of the truck and cranks up the engine, which coughs several times before it starts.

With its first jerk forward, Pablito rolls backwards like a ball, Mama cries out and I bump my elbow against a metal tool box. As we bounce, I manage to grab Pablito and pull him over to Mama, where I put her skirt into his little fist. "Hold here, Pablito." We will all die from this ride, I think, as I hold tightly to Pablito and to the rail of the truck.

The road soon becomes smoother and the man drives even faster. The wind slaps my wet hair against my face and Mama cries out in pain. I call to her, but she does not speak. Pablito hugs her body for warmth and I decide to do the same. I put my arms around her waist and touch a lump. It is the pouch tied under her skirt. I decide that it must be important or she would not have hid it, so I lift her skirt and undo the pouch, then retie the rough leather straps under my own skirt.

The truck streaks past a wire fence and pulls to a stop in front of an old wooden farm house. There are no lights from within. The man jumps from the truck and bangs on the door, then he hurries back to Mama. "Come, señora," he mutters. "Perhaps Doña Anita can help you."

A bulky woman, carrying a small lantern, steps out onto the porch. Her massive body is covered by a long white gown. She quickly raises the lantern and peers out. I can see one big eye that opens and shuts like that of an owl, and I grab Mama tightly.

"Eh? What goes on here?" asks the woman.

"Doña Anita, this woman was hurt crossing the river. Do what you can for her. These are her children. I must return to the river for my compadre, because he waits to see if her husband makes it across."

"Ah . . . Chente! The things you get into! What am I going to do with the little ones if she dies?" she shouts.

"We will worry about that later. That I promise, Doña Anita. I shall return." He makes the sign of the cross upon his heart, then races to the truck, which coughs and sputters as it speeds out of sight.

The woman has no trouble carrying Mama into the house. I follow with Pablito. She grumbles as she lays Mama on the only bed in the room, then she motions for us to sit in the corner. As I move to the dark corner, she throws a blanket which hits me on the back of the head. I pick it up and pull Pablito over to the corner.

For a few minutes Pablito sits quietly beside me, staring at the woman's giant shadow against the bare wall. When he falls asleep, I leave him and go over to the bed to see what this horrid woman is doing to Mama.

"She's a pretty one," she mutters as she removes Mama's wet clothes.

I watch her every move. Into her hands she rubs a smelly lotion, then with her thick fingers she digs into the wound and blood flows out. She presses harder and the blood trickles down Mama's side. She picks up another bottle and pours it over the blood, and then she sighs heavily. I do not like the idea of this strange woman touching Mama.

She stops working and stares at me. "Be of use, girl! Get me a pail of water. Move!" Her fowl breath almost knocks me over, but I cross my arms and refuse to move. "No!"

"You want your Mama to live?" she asks. Her twisted face makes my heart jump to my throat. Frightened, I turn to where she points. I find a pail of water much too heavy, so I take a small pan and fill it. I return and hand her the water and it is then that I notice that she has removed all of Mama's clothing. She covers her with a blanket. I look at Mama's clothes heaped on the floor and I feel I should hang them neatly so that they will be dry for her to wear in the morning.

The woman pulls the lantern closer and hunches over Mama. "Ah, the shot went through. It's good, if she has not lost too much blood." She holds out her hand and orders, "Give me a towel, a wet one."

I stare at Mama's wound, which seems to be a small hole, all swollen and blue. "Shot? Did you say shot?" I stammer.

"Yes. Now, will you give me a towel!"

I start to shake and then I scream, "Mama will die!"

She moves around the bed and slaps my face. It stings like a thousand bees attacking me. "Girl! Stop it! I need your help. Get control of yourself and give me that towel!"

Her shouts move me into action. I must help Mama. "Si, yes, señora!" I turn to fetch the towel.

I stand watching the old one work. Her hands move rapidly from one jar to another and never seem to stop. I marvel at her speed for such a fat woman. Occasionally, she closes both eyes and bends down to listen to Mama's chest, then she grunts as if she were about to throw up. Never once does she look up from her work, and I watch very closely as her healing hands tend to Mama's wound. She truly has a gift from God, I decide.

"Hand me that whisky that sits on the table!"

I fetch it and watch as she pours it over the wound and over the pricks that scar Mama's arm.

"That should do it. Now, all we have to do is pray." She bandages the wound. "Do you know how to pray, girl?"

"A little," I mutter, backing away from the breeze of her stinking breath and the ugly blood-shot, blinking eye.

"Good. You must pray for your Mama," she snaps while wiping her hands on her skirt.

I have Mama's beads, so I go to the corner to pray. "Hail Mary, full of grace," I say over and over until I cannot remember a thing.

It is the crowing of the rooster that wakes me to find Pablito sitting on the old one's lap, eating a tortilla. The hag seems to enjoy playing with him while she urges him to eat more.

"Ah, you are awake, girl. You must have been very tired."

I rise and go over to the table. She is uglier now than last night. With one eye she stares straight at me and she stares down at Pablito with the other blinking one. It seems as though she looks two places at one time. I look away from her twisted face. "Mama? How is Mama?" I go over to the bed and Mama seems very pale in the daylight.

"She has not stirred. I forced some soup down her, but not very much. Perhaps by this evening she will come out of it."

She puts Pablito down on the floor. "Come, eat something or you will faint." She puts a plate of beans and rice on the table. Each time she moves I notice that the fat on her body swings in different directions. It seems she has no bones. She heats a tortilla and she brings it to me with a cup of hot coffee.

I eat as if I've never seen food. I want to lick the plate, but she stands there watching like a vulture. After I finish, she removes the plate and sits in the chair across from me. I shrink as far back into my chair as I dare go.

"We must talk. What's your name, girl?"

"Katarina Campos."

"Bueno. Good. I shall call you Kata. Where do you come from?"

"San Carlos, Mexico. Do you know where it is?" I ask.

"Yes, it's a little village across the border. Now you are just outside Eagle Pass, Texas."

"Do you know anything about Papa?" I blurt out.

"No, not yet. Perhaps, we shall soon hear."

I turn sideways in my chair. I do not want to cry in front of the witch, so I bite my lips hard.

"That fellow, Chente, has not returned. Such a foolish man! How much money did your Papa give them to smuggle your family across?"

"Smuggle? What is that?"

Her laughter boxes my ears and I feel faint from the sight of the grey covered eyeball which blinks open and closed.

"Girl! It's illegal to cross the border without papers. Do you have papers?"

Not knowing anything about papers, I say nothing.

"You and your family have broken the law. Do you know what that means?" She watches me like a hawk. One good eye is staring straight into me and the grey covered one is blinking rapidly. "No!" she boldly answer herself. "You are but a child, but your Mama and your Papa know! If they find you, they will send you all back to Mexico. First, you will have to spend time in jail. It's a penalty for breaking the law."

"Jail!" I shout. "Papa would not let that happen."

She rises, muttering curses to the devil, then goes out the front door carrying the pail.

How could Papa let this happen? Did he make it across the river safely? How will he know where we are? Tears fill my eyes and this time I cannot stop them from flowing. I pick up Pablito and hold him tightly. "Pablito, it's you and me . . . at least, until Mama wakes up, and I will be glad when she does." I squeeze him hard, and he cries out.

I sit on the edge of the bed, holding Mama's cold hand and staring at her frozen face in which I cannot see any movement. I pull the blankets up tighter around her and bend to kiss her cheek.

The old one mentioned papers. I remember the pouch, so I go to the door and look out to see that the witch is in the garden hoeing. I lift my skirt and undo the straps of the pouch. In it I find some paper money, a few Mexican coins that fall onto my lap and the yellow stone that the shadow so greatly admired. I take the stone and it feels rough in my fingers. It is unusual in that it has smaller rocks of a different shade planted in it. I shake the pouch, then look inside, but there are no papers with writing on them.

"What are we going to do now?" I stuff everything back into the pouch, then I tie it around my waist. I straighten my skirt and peek out to the garden where the witch is still hoeing.

Shortly, she returns to the house. She grunts as she lays the hoe against the porch, then lifts her skirt over her wrinkled ankles to enter the house. Cutting a path to Mama, she stands there studying Mama's face for several moments, then turns abruptly and motions for me to follow.

"There is no sense in wasting the day, girl. Come! There are many things to do around this ranchito."

"Like what, señora?" I ask, keeping a safe distance from her.

She stops in her tracks. "Like feeding the chickens, gathering peppers and tomatoes and then watering the garden." Her arms move in a wide sweeping motion. "And if you are still not tired by the time the sun falls, you can sweep the house."

I follow her out the rear door to the shed, where she hands me a metal pan. "Now, take this corn and go feed the chickens." She takes a handful of feed and spreads it on the ground. "Like this, see. The chicken pen is behind this shed. After all the feed is gone, gather the eggs and bring them inside."

I set about the task, understanding that we must pay for our keep in some manner. After I finish that chore, she sends me to gather green peppers and after an hour, I feel like my back has been broken into hundreds of pieces.

I take the peppers into the house, then go back to the old well to draw some cool drinking water. I throw in the old bucket that is sitting on the ledge and watch as it falls into the dark hole. It seems like many seconds pass and yards of rope fall before I hear the bucket splash down.

I start cranking the handle to bring up the bucket. It is heavy, so I lean against the edge of the well. A few loose bricks fall out of place and drop into the deep hole below. Frightened, I let go of the crank. The crank begins to spin rapidly and it knocks me backwards onto the ground. I rise and shake the dust off my skirt and decide that the drink will have to wait.

"Kata!" she screams. "While you are out there, pull up a potato or two for supper."

"Where are they?" I scream back.

"In the garden, girl. Where else would they be?"

I look over the rows of plants. I cannot find the potatoes, so I go up to the back porch. "I do not know which is the potato plant."

"That girl does not know a potato plant from a sunflower. May the Lord have mercy on her inexperienced soul. But she is lucky, for I will teach her many things while she stays with me."

I bow my head, feeling very foolish, but I do not say I am sorry. She slams the screen door, then passes me in a huff, so much so that her skirt seems to slap me in the face.

I follow her to the potato plants and watch as she digs deep into the earth. "Watch, girl. It is not hard to find potatoes. Now, see if you can bring me in four or five for our supper." As she rises and turns, her skirt seems to fan out and throw dirt at me.

Later, we sit around the table, eating supper. Pablito sits on her lap and giggles. He likes her, but I am not so comfortable, so I glance across the room to Mama, who still sleeps.

"Perhaps tomorrow she will wake up," she says in a much softer voice than she had used all day.

Our eyes meet. Her good one is red-brown and narrow like a speck. Her bad one is grey-blue, almost cloud-like. Her hair is red-brown mixed with much gray. It almost looks dead.

"What is your name?" I ask bravely.

"Anita. Anita Morales."

"Have you no children?"

"I have no need for children!" she answers sharply.

I feel as if she has slapped me again. I ask no further questions. I just eat my beans in silence, watching her and Pablito play together. Perhaps she likes boys instead of girls. Maybe it is because he's still a baby and everyone loves babies. That's why she likes him, I decide, because he's harmless and loveable.

A sharp knock pierces the room and I jump out of my chair. Again the knock, but this time much harder.

Anita motions for me to remain quiet, then she walks over to the door. "Who is it"

"Chente. Please, Doña Anita, open up!"

"Ah, you foolish man. You're more trouble than your hide is worth!" She curses under breath, then opens the door to let him step inside.

He stoops as he comes through the door. Then he removes his hat and stands waiting for Anita to invite him further into the house. Anita stands rooted and does not speak. Her arms are crossed over her huge hanging breasts.

He glances over at Mama, then nods to me before he speaks. "We have not found him, señora. Our fear is that he was shot and has floated downstream. We could not even find his guitar. There are many agents covering the area, making it impossible for us to get any closer."

"You mulehead!" shouts Anita.

"Yes, señora. My compadre and I are going into hiding until things cool off!"

"You donkey! What am I to do with these children and that sick woman?" Anita grabs him by the collar and pulls him to her.

He closes his eyes and turns his face as Anita blows her fowl breath into his nose. He shrugs slightly, offering no suggestions. "I cannot say, señora."

"A donkey's ass! You must pay me for their keep. The woman is sick and cannot work or travel. She could die! What if they check this place?" She releases his shirt and throws him against the closed door.

"I think not, señora. We will not betray you." He bends at the knees slowly to pick up his hat. "Besides, no one ever comes out here."

Anita steps toward him and he shrinks against the door in fear. "Give me money, you goat of Satan! Or I will put a curse on you that will never be removed!" Her fat arms are flying all over the place, and her fingers seem to turn into sharp thorns as she approaches him. The man appears faint, but he does not take his eyes off her.

I cry out, knowing that she does not want us or our troubles, but I do not care. I fall to my knees on hearing that Papa is gone and shall never return. It is as if I have been pierced by a sharp arrow dipped in poison. Tears flow and I cover my eyes and mouth with my hands. Pablito comes over to me and leans against me for comfort, but I still shake and gasp for air.

Chapter Three

With shaking hands, the man reaches into his shirt pocket and pulls out a roll of bills from which he takes three and hands them to Anita.

"Stupid!" yells Anita at the top of her lungs. She suddenly lunges forward and yanks the roll out of his hands. "Get out of my sight!" she warns.

The man stumbles out the door and hurries to the truck. Anita jerks open the door and chases after him, raging like a mad bull.

The shouting and cursing frightens Pablito and he begins to cry. I try to calm him, but as miracles go, his violent cries enter Mama's ears. She gasps, then moans loudly. Her eyes flutter open as she turns slowly to search the room for us.

"Kata? Pablito? Where are you? Where is Carlos?"

I pick up Pablito and rush to the bed. "Here, Mama!"

"Thank the Lord!" She reaches out to touch my hand, but the pain in her arm shoots out. She recoils like a snake.

"Be still, señora. You should not move. You need rest."

Mama's eyes dart toward Anita and searches Anita's face for recognition. "I do not know you."

"You are in my home. You were brought here last night by some men, the kind that look for easy money. Fear not, the scoundrels shall be punished. I have put a curse on them."

"Carlos? Where is Carlos?" Mama turns to me for the answer.

I am about to tell her when the old one stares at

me with such a strong gleam that it catches my eye and mind. It is as if I am able to read her thoughts.

Anita answers, "He will return later." She glances up at me and seems to wink with her good eye. "Rest now, señora. You need your strength." She lays her fat hand over Mama's forehead, then closes both her crooked eye and her good one. She chants under her breath and Mama falls into an instant sleep.

I gasp. "Are you a witch?"

Anita roars and as quickly as the laughter began, it stops. She stares straight at me. "No, I am not a witch. I am a healer, and a seer. I work for God, not for the devil. Remember, there is a difference."

I do not want to show my ignorance, so I do not ask further questions, for I am glad for whatever miracle she has worked. She brought Mama back to me and for that I owe her much.

Anita stands and looks down at Mama. "She will be fine in a few days." She turns to the cot on which she sleeps. "Let's rest now."

That night I sleep peacefully, knowing that Mama will soon be well.

The next morning I awake to find Anita and Pablito still sleeping. I glance up at the window where the sun already shines in brightly, then I sit up and rub my eyes. I listen to Mama's breathing, which comes in and out slowly, and to Anita's mild snore. Pablito stirs, then sits up, too. He is wet, so I get a towel to change him. He coos when he feels the dry towel between his legs, then he smiles happily.

"Hush, Pablito. The old one is still sleeping," I whisper.

Anita turns in her cot. "No, I am not sleeping, only resting." The cot squeaks as she sits up. "Today is

"Oh, no. You know it's true, woman. You have a fine reputation for healing with all your herbs and tonics."

"Don Juan, you are making a mountain out of all this. I insist that you shut your mouth." She lifts a pot from the stove and puts it on the table.

He smiles, showing his grey teeth. "What's for dinner, my dear woman?"

He pats her behind and she pushes him away. "Get away, man!" she warns as she lifts the spoon to his head.

Mama and I laugh and they both turn red as ripe tomatoes. Anita starts laughing when she sees Pablito clinging to Don Juan's leg, trying to taste it.

During supper, I notice that Anita seems nice with Don Juan around. She enjoys watching him eat his food, as if he hadn't eaten all week long.

After supper Anita and Don Juan sit on the porch and talk as they watch the sun go down. Pablito crawls in and out between their legs and they do not seem to mind.

Much later Don Juan enters the room to say goodnight to Mama. "I will go into town to check the jails to see if your husband is there. Anita wishes me to do that for you, and I owe her many favors. Besides, there could be trouble if you go, since you are not from these parts."

"I understand, Don Juan, and I appreciate your kindness."

He bows low and puts on his floppy straw hat. "See you later, children." He goes outside to the old truck and cranks it up. It whines, then stops. "Come on, old blue. Don't let me down now," he demands. The engine cranks up and sputters as he turns out of the yard. "See you old girl!" he shouts to Anita.

Before we go to bed, Anita approaches Mama and asks about her plans. Mama shakes her head and says, "I have no idea what to do." Anita sits on the edge of the bed. "If need be," continues Mama, "I can get a job as a dishwasher in the town. I know we are a burden to you and I appreciate your help."

"You are only a tiny burden in comparison to the rest of the world's problems. Besides, I enjoy the boy and those rascals that got you into this mess helped by giving me money." From between her breasts she pulls out a roll of bills. "Here. It's yours and the children's. You will need it to find a place to stay in town."

"Oh, I cannot take the money. It's rightfully yours for tending to us."

"What use have I for money? I seldom get into town." Anita thrusts the bills into Mama's hands.

"You are kind, señora. How will we ever repay you?"

"Oh, I do have one weakness. You can repay me by sending me postcards from wherever you go. For me, they are proof that beautiful places exist in this world. Look!" She pulls out a brown sack from a drawer. "They come by mail and it's like Christmas each time I receive one."

I take the sack from her. "There's bunches of them!" I pour them out onto Mama's lap.

"See!" Anita continues, "they come from Dallas, El Paso and Austin. I even have one from Santa Fe, New Mexico. It's from a man who came to see me with a snake bite that was all swollen and infected. I cured him."

"I cannot believe that there are such places," gasps Mama.

Anita slaps her thigh. "I told you! Don Ramon brings them in the mail. He stops for a cup of coffee and reads them to me. I have learned what all of them say from memory."

"Such wonderous places!" I cry.

"Yes, Kata. I tell you, every Sunday night I go through them. It's like I'm visiting those places on a trip. Can you picture a miserable old woman like me walking down such streets?"

I looked up to see a dream-like haze cover Anita's face. But I cannot picture her dressed in a shabby skirt walking down such streets. Nor can I see myself doing so. I notice that the same distant glow that lights up Anita's face has also captured Mama's.

"If only Carlos could see these cards. He told me such places existed, but I doubted him. I called him a dreamer, but he only wanted us to better ourselves," says Mama.

"Perhaps," chuckles Anita.

"He heard that there are jobs that pay good wages. He said that there was free education for the little ones and I doubted it all."

Anita pats Mama's shoulder. "Those are his dreams. A man's dreams are always different from a woman's because they think of themselves first, then they think of the needs of the family. The power of dreams is indeed great, but only as great as the person who dreams them."

"Why do you know so much about dreams?" I ask, not making much sense out of her rattling on in such a way.

She rises, goes over to the closet and she pulls out a small book. "This is a dream book and it tells all about dreams and their outcome. I have studied it faithfully, because I feel it is part of every person alive."

Mama takes the book from her hand. "Where did you get this?"

"Another person I cured sent it to me through the mail." Anita takes the book from Mama. "It's from Mexico City. See, it has no words, just pictures. It is easy to understand, no?" She takes the book and puts it back in the closet. "Dreams are something one takes seriously." She gathers the post cards and puts them back into their sack. "Tomorrow is another day filled with who knows what. Let's go to bed, now." She straightens Mama's blanket, then tucks us in.

That night I toss and turn, unable to sleep. I lay awake thinking about those postcards. If such places exist, then it must be a very large world, much larger than I ever imagined. Mama called Papa a dreamer. Would he be foolish enough to risk sending us to jail for those places?

That night I dream of Papa, whose face is caught in a rain cloud. Tears stream down his face and he keeps yelling something, but I cannot make out what he says. My heart aches like a pin cushion stuck a thousand times over because I cannot help him and there's nothing I can do to find him.

Several days later Mama catches a ride into town with Don Juan. She waves goodbye from the cab of the Model-T as it rambles slowly onward.

All day I wait for her to return.

"Kata! You will never finish the chores if you do not stop searching the road."

"Yes, Anita. Why isn't she back?" I look toward the setting sun.

"She will be, soon enough. Don Juan will return by nightfall and there's still plenty of daylight left.

Perhaps he had some extra marketing to do."

I do not believe her answer, but I go back to my chores with my fingers crossed and every now and then I glance up the road.

After supper Anita hums a tune. I can tell by her peeking looks out the window that she is getting worried. "My goodness, I hope that old truck has not overheated again. Don Juan knows nothing about trucks. He just points them down the road."

I clean the tin plates with water from the well, then set them upside down to dry. I sigh, realizing it is time for bed and still Mama has not returned.

Anita does not turn out the lantern and I am thankful, for it will serve as a guide for Mama. As tired as I am, I fight sleep. I glance at Anita, who sits on her cot and stares at the door. She is worried because usually by this hour every night she is snoring. Sleep finally overtakes me.

The rattling of the pans wakes me and I sit up and search the room, but Mama is not there. Her cot has not been touched. Anita looks my way. "She'll be back today. I can feel it in my old bones. Come! Have some breakfast, for there's a long work day ahead."

I step to the porch and wash my face in the round tub, then glare at the road leading to town. The empty ache inside my belly will not accept her tardiness. I hang the paper thin towel back on the nail and go inside to eat. A big appetite will please old Anita.

"Has Pablito eaten?" I ask.

"Yes, long ago."

As I eat scrambled eggs and corn tortillas I hear only the sounds of my teeth grinding. I cannot bear the silence any longer. "Anita," I ask, "what will become of us if Mama does not come back?"

Anita turns and then chuckles softly, "I told you she will come back."

"But, what if she doesn't, just like Papa?"

"You must have faith, little one."

I shove my plate away and bury my head in my arms. "What is faith, Anita? I need my Mama and my Papa!" I wail, not caring if she sees me cry.

After I cry awhile, I feel her hand on my head. "Faith is power, little one. Do not worry, for she will return. Besides, you and Pablito are welcome to live here with me, if she does not come back."

I seize her hand. "What do you mean, if she does not come back?" I gasp.

Anita takes both my hands in hers, "She will come back, girl. I tell you and you must believe in what I say!"

"Anita, you ... mean that ... we can stay here with you? We can live here? Oh, Anita. I always thought you were a bad person, but you're not and I have gone out of my way to make it hard on you."

She crushes me to her belly. "You are not the first person to think that, Kata. It's all right, for I am an ugly old woman set on having my way and helping others in my own way. I get lonely at times, but you and Pablito have eased my loneliness."

"I'll be your friend, forever," I vow as I kiss her hand.

She dries my tears with the corner of her apron and chuckles, "Forever is such a long, long time, Kata. But, you are welcome here forever."

Chapter Four

After lunch Anita sends me to water the garden. After an hour or so I glance up from my fork to see a stranger upon a horse turn into the gate. He slumps in the saddle as the horse moves along at a slow pace. I throw the bucket down and run into the house shouting, "Anita, someone comes!"

She hurries out to the porch and on seeing the man runs to his aid. She leads the horse to the house, then pulls the man off and lays him upon the porch. With her two thumbs she yanks back his eyelids and peers deeply into his eyes.

She makes a throaty clicking sound, then mutters, "I do not see what is wrong with him." She quickly unties his clothes, checks his chest, his arms and his back. "Go inside, Kata, and bring me a blanket."

She removes all his clothing and piles it on top of the man, covering his private parts. In one quick flick of the wrists, she spreads the blanket over him. "Water, Kata. Hurry!"

I race to the well and throw in the bucket. While I crank the bucket up, more stones fall into the deep well. I pay no attention. Instead, I race back to Anita with the pail full of water. I find Anita bending over him with her ear on his hairy chest.

"Kata, get my tray full of herbs."

I do as she asks and set the tray down within her reach. "What's wrong with him?"

She glances up at me. "Yes, I believe it is time for you to start learning about herbs." She winks, then lifts his right hand to spread his fingers wide. "Look, two small pricks that will start swelling. Perhaps, a snake bite or a tarantula's bite. It doesn't matter, because the remedy is the same for both."

"Why is he sleeping?" I ask, staring down at the man's open mouth.

Anita laughs and pats her stomach. "He probably thought he would die, so he got himself drunk. For men, death is painless that way. Watch, I'll give him a drop or two of this on his tongue and it'll snap him out of his sleep."

As soon as the drops hit his tongue, the man jerks into a sitting position. "Que? What?" He realizes that he has no clothes on and yanks the blanket up to his chest.

"Don Paz, what is your problem?" drills Anita, who stands with her hands on her hips.

He lifts his hand to her nose. "Something bit me and I know not what. So, I came as quickly as I could."

Anita roars and slaps him hard on the back. "You were too drunk to know what bit you, but I assure you that, with God's help, you will live one more day."

"Gracias, Doña Anita," he says, wiping his mouth with the back of his hand.

"I will make a paste to cover the bite and draw out any poison."

"I will be in your debt, Doña Anita," he sighs in relief.

"You are already in my debt, Don Paz," declares Anita as she turns for the tray. "Kata, watch me as I make this paste."

I stand close to her and watch as she takes a white powder and explains, "This is a fine ground wheat and this is squeezed root onion. I shall mix them together, then add this brown liquid which comes from a secret root of which you shall learn about later."

The odor is unbearable, so I hold my nose and watch as she rubs the paste into the bites. Don Paz jumps, but she holds him still.

"Do not rub so hard, señora!" shouts Don Paz, who almost slaps Anita's hand.

"You are the one that needs to be slapped around very hard, Don Paz! Get dressed, then you may leave!" she commands. "We will go into the house to allow you some privacy." She lifts her tray to her shoulder, then follows me into the house.

"Will he be all right?" I ask.

"He will be fine, Kata. My paste has never failed."

Soon Don Paz knocks at the door. "Doña Anita, may I leave this bottle of whisky for you as payment?" he begs.

Anita goes out to the porch. "Many thanks, Don Paz, and go with God!" She smiles, then bows to him.

Don Paz backs off the porch clutching his hat and turns quickly to mount his horse. He wastes no time in galloping out of the gate.

That afternoon I am hoeing in the corn patch when I see dust rising from the road. I stand with the hoe in hand, blocking the sun from my eyes with the other hand. I see a vehicle that approaches slowly, so I drop everything and run to meet it.

"Mama! Welcome back!" I shout. I stop in front of her. "Oh, Mama! That is the most beautiful skirt I have ever seen."

"Do you like it, Kata? I hated to spend the money, but in town one must look decent, especially when looking for a job." She holds the skirt out and circles around.

"You needed a new skirt, Mama."

She falls on her knees to hug me. "I missed you, Katarina. I have a little present for you and for Pablito."

"Pablito! Where are you?" I shout, glancing around.

Mama enters the house and greets Anita, who is preparing tacos and a drink for Don Juan. I follow at their heels, eager to hear the news.

"Anita," says Mama, "we are back at last. With your blessing, I have found a job as a seamstress and Don Juan knows the lady for whom I am to work. It is good, no?"

"Ah, at long last Don Juan has the privilege of re-paying his duties to mankind. It is just," grins Anita.

Don Juan removes his hat and smiles, "I always try to help. You know that, dear Anita."

"I know, Don Juan. It just takes you a long time to figure out how to be of help. That's all," snaps Anita.

Mama turns to me, "Kata, go fetch Pablito."

I turn and run outside. I run completely around the house and I do not see him, so I run back into the house. "I cannot find Pablito."

"What!" gasps Mama. "Surely, he's around here some place."

All of us hurry out the back door. Mama leads while I follow, but I glance back to see that Anita and Don Juan are stuck together in the door.

"Move man, or I shall clobber you!" shouts Anita.

"Be calm, Anita dear. The madder you get, the harder it is for me to slip through."

"Pablito!" shouts Mama. "Baby, come to Mama!"

I hear him cry softly like a kitten, so I run to the outhouse, thinking he might be playing behind it. He is not there, so I turn and look toward the well. I see many stones lying loosely on the ground and then I notice a hole in the wall. It had not been there before. "Mama! Anita!" I shout. "Come, look!" I point to the well wall.

Anita runs over and sticks her head down into the well. "Pablito!" she calls.

Don Juan pulls her back. "Get away woman or you shall be down there!" With one great heave he moves her out of the way, then he climbs to the top of the rail to peer down into the well. "Yes, I see something, but I need my flashlight from the truck."

"I'll get it, Don Juan." I tear across the garden, leaping rows of plants. When I return, I am breathless. "Here."

Don Juan hangs onto the rope with one hand, then flicks on the light with the other. Again I hear a small cry that seems to echo from within the well.

"My baby, my baby!" screams Mama.

Anita grabs her and hugs her tightly. "Be calm. We shall get him up. Be thankful that since we can hear him cry, we know he is alive, and that I will be able to work with him."

Don Juan jumps off the well and races to the front of the house. He drives his old truck over the garden, smashing the plants, and parks it as close to the well wall as he dares. From the bed of the truck he pulls a long rope and ties it to the front bumper. "It is a good thing I bought this rope at the market," he says. "Anita, hold here," he commands, "and see to it that the knot does not come loose."

"What are you going to do, you old fool!" she asks.

He glances up at her. "Something you could not do, my dear."

I hug Mama and watch as Don Juan lowers himself into the well. Between his teeth he holds the flashlight. Anita holds tightly to the rope. The seconds seem like hours and soon Anita wails, "I should have had the old thing fixed. It's all my fault. Now I will never forgive myself!"

Mama cries harder and I hug her waist, trying to comfort her. "Hail Mary, Mother of God," she says over and over.

"Old woman!" shouts Don Juan, "I found him on a small ledge. He is very muddy and I cannot tell if he is hurt. Now, hold tight, for I am coming up with him."

"Thanks to the Lord!" Anita crosses herself. The rope seems to strain under their weight. Anita holds as tight as she can. Her bad eye is flicking at such a fast pace that my eyes start to flick too.

Suddenly, she lets go of the rope and jumps into the truck which she quickly cranks up. The truck moves into reverse as it slowly pulls them up.

The top of Don Juan's head appears first. He is very red in the face and seems to gasp for breath, but he manages to throw the flashlight out. He has Pablito tucked inside his shirt with his belt securely knotted around the baby's waist. Pablito has fainted and is as pale as Anita's powders.

Mama runs to help him. I gasp as I watch her stretch herself out over the well in order to take Pablito.

"No!" commands Don Juan. "Take the rope and pull us in."

Mama pulls at the end of the rope and Don Juan, in one great lunge, lands with his feet on the ground, then falls onto his back. He sits up and unties the baby, then hands him to Mama, who rushes him inside the house. Anita hurries after her.

Don Juan sits with his legs crossed upon the ground. He rubs the sweat off his forehead. I rush to hug him. "Thank you, Don Juan. You saved my little brother."

"I would have given my life for that boy."

I kiss him on the cheek and he turns very red. I help him to his feet and watch as he slowly puts his hat upon his head. Then, he glances up and his eyes open wide.

"Oh, no!" he gasps. "What have I done to Anita's little garden? She will never forgive me."

I take his hand and kiss his palm. "Yes, she will forgive you, because you saved Pablito."

He smiles down at me. "Maybe you're right, child. I hope so, or she will never cook for me again," he says, shaking the dirt from his white pants.

That night Anita fixes a special treat in celebration of Mama's return and Pablito's rescue. I lick my lips, watching her as she fries tortillas and coats them heavily with sugar.

My days at the ranchito are simple. I do the same chores day after day and each night I fall into bed exhausted from the toil. Pablito follows me, adding to my misery. If I am feeding the chickens, he is chasing them away. If I am watering the garden, he knocks the water bucket over, and if I am picking tomatoes, he picks the ones that are not ripe. I yell at him, but he does not mind me.

Anita and I sweat beneath our clothes, but we talk as we hoe the garden or cook our simple meals. We have become close friends as she teaches me about

41

herbs and healing and her strong faith. I have seen her heal snake bites, bee stings, even broken legs on a dog that wandered into the ranchito. She is indeed a healer.

Mama announces one weekend that she has found a place for us to live in town. As she describes the room with its own tiny bathroom, tears come to Anita's eyes. I will miss Anita greatly, but for me the work at the ranchito never ends. I see few rewards in working myself so hard.

"Anita," I suggest, "why don't you sell this place and come with us to town?"

She dries her tears on the corner of her apron. "This is my home. It has been in my family for years and I cannot sell it. My father would turn in his grave at the thought."

"But Anita, what will become of the place once you are gone?"

"I will worry about that later. Besides, what would I do all day in town? Gossip here and gossip there? Where will I find my herbs? No, I cannot accept your offer, as kind as it is." Her chin quivers as she stares down at her untouched supper.

"Anita," I say, "I know you want to come. You must come. We need you as much as you need us. You are alone out here, except for Don Juan." I hug her massive shoulders, trying to win her over, for I know that I will be very afraid without her.

She pats my arm. "No, I cannot go. You will learn to survive without me. I will have to learn to do without you and your brother." She glances down at her plate and stirs her beans. Her bad eye blinks rapidly. "Besides, I will come visit you on weekends. Would you like that?"

"I'd love it!" I shout, hugging her again.

Mama sighs, "As you wish, Anita." She takes her plate to the stove. "I still have not heard anything about Carlos. I went with Don Juan to check the lists posted at the jailhouse, but his name is not on it." She sighs, then sits herself down again. "When I have a chance, I go to the front door of the shop and watch the streets, hoping that he might pass."

"Have you checked the market on the other side of town?" questions Anita.

"No, not yet. Perhaps when we have settled I will have more time to search the town and ask more questions."

"If he has been in town, someone there will have seen him. If he has drowned in the river, it will be posted outside the police station. We will check again." Anita rises. "My friends will tell me if they have seen him."

"I hope you are right, Anita," whispers Mama.

"Mama," I ask, "tell me, do you still like your job?"

She smiles at me. "It is fine and I only work as hard as I have to. The wage is small and the hours are long. Thank goodness, I will have you to look after Pablito while I am at work."

"I will make a good babysitter," I add.

"Good. Because we must help one another, especially since Anita will not be along."

"And, I will cook and clean so you won't have to."

Mama brushes my hair back. "That's my big girl."

Anita touches my shoulder. "Remember, Kata, never let a stranger into the room. Some people want to do harm to others for no reason other than the devil tempts them."

"I'll remember, Anita," I say taking her hand in mine.

"Good. Tomorrow is Saturday and we will wash the clothes so that they will be clean for packing."

"I will help draw the water," I add.

Anita rises. "No, I will draw all the water we need until Don Juan takes the time to fix that old well."

"But, what can I do?" I ask.

She stops and turns, "You may hang the clothes on the line to dry."

"Okay, Anita. That's much more fun than drawing water."

Mama rises. "It's time for bed." She hands me a blanket, which I take to our bed of straw.

The minute I lay my head down I start dreaming. I remember Anita turning out the lantern. I see the moonlight peek through the window, but I don't remember how that man enters my dreams.

The man comes walking out of a cloud. He seems to be in a big hurry and trudges forward with heavy steps. His boots are like a cowboy's and very muddy. I see that his shirt sleeves are rolled up past his elbows, as if he has just gotten off a dirty job. On his right arm is a tattoo of a lady with a snake wrapped around her waist.

He approaches a bolted door which is painted blue. He pushes at the door with all his weight, but it does not give. After several tries the man steps back and doubles up his fists. I see myself standing on the other side of the door. I am shaking with terror. His fist smashes through the door and the arm with the naked lady slowly reaches inside and unbolts the door. Helpless, I fall to my knees and raise my arms to protect myself from flying wood. I faint as the door creeps open.

I awake screaming. Mama is holding me and

Anita stands behind her with a lighted candle. Pablito sits up rubbing his eyes, but I hold tightly to Mama, as if I were once again drowning.

Mama rocks me back and forth in comfort. "She is frightened of a dream," she whispers to Anita.

"What did you dream, Kata?" asks Anita as she sets the candle down and hurries to the closet. There she pulls out her book. "This is my dream book and you must tell me what you dreamed while you can remember it, Kata."

"Oh, Anita. It's just a child's dream!" scolds Mama.

"Dreams are signs, and we must listen to them at all times. Now, Kata. Tell me quickly."

I sit up watching as she leafs through the book. I tell her what I have seen as I floated above the dream like an angel.

She grumbles as she flips the pages rapidly. "Naked lady with a snake around her waist . . . that means that a woman will be hurt. That is bad." She flips more pages.

"It is just a bad dream, Anita. Do not worry," Mama assures her, but Anita pays no attention.

"The blue painted door means that it was placed there for protection against evil. Blue is the color of the heavens. That is a good sign," says Anita with a slight smile.

"But, Anita," I ask,"why am I an angel floating like a cloud, yet able to see everything?"

"Ah . . . that is the best sign. It means that someone will arrive to protect you from harm." She quickly turns more pages and her smile disappears. "The first means that the man wants something you have in your possession. That is very bad." She closes the book and sits staring out into space.

Mama goes over to Anita. "I do not believe in that silly book."

Anita quickly glances up and brushes back her grey hair. "You should believe it, señora. For the book comes from your very land."

"So, what does that matter?" snaps Mama.

"Oh, I fear for the children!" moans Anita, rocking herself back and forth. "How I fear for their lives. Leave them with me while you work. Let us continue as we are. Does the arrangement not suit everyone?" Anita wails.

"No, not me. I miss the children. I need to see them every day, not just on weekends." Mama falls on her knees before Anita. "Don't you understand, Anita, I need them more than you."

"You are the one that fails to see. You keep them for selfish reasons, while I keep them for their own good," Anita snaps as she rises. "Beware of dreams, señora. Do not take them lightly."

"Anita, I know you mean well, but let's not argue just because I don't believe in your book."

Anita slowly lies down upon her cot and stares upward at the ceiling for several moments. She clears her throat before she answers, "I am your friend, but I do take the liberty of warning you of these things, and I worry for the children's sake as well as your own."

Mama stiffens as if she has been struck. "Anita, por favor, let's not speak of this dream anymore." She walks over to me and tucks me in, then goes back to her bed.

"As you wish, señora," adds Anita as she turns her face to the wall.

"Leave the candle on, Mama," I ask feeling very frightened and confused.

Chapter Five

Early in the morning I rise and go the the out-house where I check the pouch, making sure that the straps are secure around my waist. Then I walk to the front of the house and sit on the porch, watching the road for Don Juan, who is very late. I am anxious to get into to town to see our new home, and his lateness angers me as well as Anita, who grumbles loudly as she puts a sack full of vegetables down on the steps.

"That old fool is forever taking his blessed time!" she snorts.

I glance up at her. "He will come, Anita. You must be nice to Don Juan. He likes you."

She spins around. "He likes my cooking, not me, Kata. All men love women that cook good meals. That is why they are led around by their stomachs rather than by their hearts." She smoothes her apron and peers into the distance.

I laugh. "I know you like him too, Anita. You can't fool me."

Anita growls, "What does a child like you know about men?"

"Only what I see," I answer. "Look! Don Juan comes now."

"Well, it's about time!" she snaps as she goes back into the house.

I help Don Juan load all the things into the back of the truck and then I turn to Anita, who stands with her hands crossed over her chest, as if she does not know what to do. "Anita!" I cry, "I shall miss you and this ranchito." I jump off the bed of the truck and fly into her arms for a moment of comfort.

"My dear, little Kata. Remember, you are welcome here forever." She hugs me tightly, then she takes Pablito into her arms and kisses him furiously.

Mama comes out on the porch and she too embraces Anita. "Thank you for everything, Anita."

"Take care of the little ones." Anita's body shakes in great sobs as she hugs Mama again. "God be with you and the children."

I climb into the back of the truck and sit on a bale of hay. Mama and Pablito climb in front with Don Juan. Anita starts waving goodbye when the truck starts. We pass through the gates and I glance back to see that she has taken off her apron and waves it wildly in the air.

The truck stops in front of an old two story house. Don Juan climbs out and says, "This is the place, señora." He holds the door open for Mama, then reaches inside the truck to take Pablito.

I stand up in the back of the truck and stare at the huge house with its crumbling steps and its stove pipe chimneys. "Mama," I say, "the first strong wind that comes along will knock this place down."

"Oh, Kata! Don't be silly!" she scolds. "Now, hop down so we can go inside."

The porch squeaks and groans as it complains of our weight and Don Juan almost pulls the door knob from the door. "This place needs lots of work," he says as he stands aside to let Mama through.

Mama takes a key with a number on it from her bundle. It matches with the number on the door at the top of the stairs. She puts the key in the lock and turns the knob. "Well, we're here at last."

Our new home is an upstairs room which has two mattresses on the floor. It has a closet-size bath and thin walls and one large window that overlooks the busy street below. The glass in the window is stained yellow with age. I try to rub it clean with my hand, but it does not help.

The tub has animal claws for feet. "Mama, this tub is rusty." I open the faucet. The water runs out dirty until at long last it clears somewhat. I take a sip, then spit it out. "This water tastes ugly! I would rather drink the cool well water at Anita's than this muddy water."

Mama swings around to me as if she wants to strike out. "Kata! We will fix this place later."

I circle the room. "But Mama, there's not even a place to cook."

She sighs, "I will go to the market and buy a hot plate. That will do for now." She smiles weakly. "We'll figure out some way to make tortillas on it."

Don Juan interrupts, "I must leave, señora. Good luck." He tips his hat and says, "I am sure we will see each other again."

I hear the old truck crank up from the street below and dash over to the window. "Goodbye, Don Juan! Take care of Anita!" I shout.

He waves his hat from the window, then disappears around the corner. I turn to see Mama sitting on the lumpy mattress in the center of the room. Her shoulders droop to her knees and she rubs her neck as if it hurts. She is tired and I do not want to upset her anymore, so I add, "Mama, we can paint the room to brighten it up." She stops rubbing her neck and smiles up at me.

That night we are all restless. It is not the brilliant moon that flows in through the glass, but a street light which casts yellow shadows against the bare walls. Nor is it quiet, like out at the ranchito. The trucks and cars honk and the wagon wheels rattle over the stone street late into the night, and I hear Mama's beads as the pass through her fingers.

I am not comfortable at our new home. Pablito does not seem to mind the change, as long as I take him outside for long afternoon walks. For me, the room grows ever so small, as if the walls are closing in on top of me, and I cannot stop them.

I enjoy the afternoon walks because they make the day shorter. Often we sit on the steps and watch people pass. I study them silently. Is he a farmer? Or does he work in a laundry? How many children does she have? It's a game I play with myself because I never speak to these people. I only wave if they wave at me.

On the fourth night that we spend in our room, I awake covered in sweat. I sit up quickly and turn to Mama, but she sleeps so soundly that I decide not to disturb her. I lay quietly in the dark, wondering why the man with the tattoo has once again awakened me from my sleep.

I rise and walk over to the window to look out. Far below, I see a man standing beneath the street lamp, smoking a cigarette. He seems lost, so I watch him for several moments, but soon he walks into the darkness around the corner.

The next afternoon I take Pablito for his usual walk around the block. As I turn the corner I stop and gasp, for I see the man with the tattoo. "Pablito! Come here quickly!" I take his hand and hurry in the direction of our room. A cold chill springs up my back and the man turns quickly, as if he has recognized me.

At the next corner I glance back to find that he is

following us at a very slow pace. He stops for a moment to scratch his head, but never takes his eyes off us. I hurry Pablito back toward the house, but in a final burst of speed the man runs towards us. I drag Pablito as fast as I can, but the man passes us, then stops in front of the apartment house. There on the steps several yards from us he turns and stares at me in a hard way. Then he disappears through the door.

I wait outside for a long time until Pablito becomes cranky from the hot afternoon sun. "Oh, Pablito. I am scared. I do not want to go inside, but you need to take your nap and I must be brave."

Once I step inside I see no one around, so I rush upstairs. I put the key to our door and fly through it bolting it securely behind me. I back away from the door slowly, trying to remember what Anita said about bad signs. I put Pablito on the mattress and sit for a moment trying to catch my breath. A light tap on the door makes my skin jump and after a long time I stammer, "Who is it?"

"Me, Anita."

"Anita!" I shout. "I'm glad you are here." I unbolt the door and rush to give her chunky figure a great hug.

"You miss me. That is good!" She chuckles, then glances at Pablito, who now lies upon the mattress half asleep.

I pull her inside and quickly bolt the door, then turn and say, "Did you have a hard time finding us?"

"No, it was fairly easy."

I give her another hard squeeze.

"My, my, barely five days. You really missed old Anita." She pushes me back gently and studies my face. "What is wrong, girl? You shake, little one."

I am about to tell her when there are loud knocks

on the door. They startle me so that I feel I have jumped right out of my sandals. Anita does not budge. I look up to her for guidance.

She stares at the door with eyes as wide as a scared cat's. She feels something, of that, I am sure. She slowly lifts one finger to her lips and motions for me to keep quiet. Again, the loud knocks crack upon the door. I see Anita glance back at the dozing Pablito and then back at the door.

"Maybe it's Mama," I whisper.

Anita seems to float magically across the floor. Once she reaches the door she starts spinning around and around, faster and faster. She stops abruptly and glares with bulging eyes, but I cannot tell if she is staring at or through the door. She makes wide sweeping motions with her hands, like half-moon shapes, then spins one way rapidly, making her skirt fan out above her knees, and then she pivots the other way very slowly and the skirt comes back down to her ankles.

A low snake hiss escapes her clinched lips and grows louder as her arms circle wide over her head. She quickly steps back and freezes, with both arms outstretched to the heavens. Deep throaty moans jump rapidly out of her neck, growing louder, then suddenly changing into low cries like those of a kitten. Then she is still and silent. Red marks seem to crease her forehead and her shoulders stiffen. Within moments the sounds of heavy footsteps move away from the door.

Anita collapses before me like a statue crumbles with age. She falls to the floor on her knees and her head hangs to her chest. Her breathing is heavy and she is covered with sweat. I run to help her, but she motions for me to let her sit for a while. I sit beside her, watching her chest and stomach heave. After a while she speaks slowly. "He will not bother you again. It was wise of you not to speak or he would have known you were here."

"Anita, why did you wave your arms like that?"

"I put the evil eye on him. Evil fights evil and he will not bother you anymore."

"How do you know, Anita?"

"Because I can see what others cannot. Evil has to be taken care of by someone who has God powers."

"But Anita! I have not been afraid all week long . . . that is until I saw him today. At first I was not sure, but I remember him from when we crossed the river, maybe it was the way he wore his sleeves."

Her smile slowly fades. "Then he wants something that you or your Mama possess." She stares into the distance for some time, then breaks into a wide smile, as if she has forgotten about the man. She pats my knee encouragingly.

"Anita, he made me feel cold all over," I add.

"That is the way your body warns you of danger. Listen to it, for it sends little messages warning us of things to happen."

"What would have happened?" I ask.

She shrugs, "Perhaps, he would have harmed you and the boy. Then your mother would have been alone in the world."

"Do you mean, kill us?"

Anita nods, then goes to Pablito, who is now stirring. I sit on the mattress and wonder how Anita knows all these things. I have heard tales in the old village of these blessed people who have powers and are capable of changing every day life with one stroke of the hand.

I watch her sitting there, bouncing Pablito up and

down. I have seen her take my mother's life in her hands and cure her. I have seen her heal like a medicine man, and I have seen her fight evil with her own hands. Yet, she is a simple woman who takes pleasure in post cards and little boys. I understand that she has much power, but I do not fear her.

Anita looks up from playing with the baby and says, "It would be best if you told your Mama about this man and what has happened here."

"If you think so, Anita. But, why worry her over nothing?"

"If you call your life nothing, then so be it. But, all mothers have a right to know the dangers that surround and befall their children."

I nod that I understand and she goes back to playing with Pablito.

When Mama arrives she greets Anita with a hug. "Thanks for coming for the weekend, Anita."

"I missed the young ones so. It is good that I came when I did, too."

"What do you mean?" questions Mama, who looks over at me.

"Mama," I blurt out, "there was a strange man knocking at the door. I believe he is the man Papa paid the money to before we crossed the river. He frightens me."

"What did he want?" She turns to Anita for the answer.

Anita hesitates, then looks at Mama closely. "Oh, I am sure it was nothing. Probably selling something. We did not answer the door."

"Good. Kata, you must never answer the door unless you know who it is. Understand?"

"Yes, Mama." I look at Anita straight in the face and she winks back at me. Perhaps Anita knows best.

After all, Mama is already biting her nails and twisting a lock of hair that has fallen forward.

"Come. I have brought fresh cheese for us and pastry for the children." Anita gently takes Mama's arm. "And a bottle of home-made wine for us señoras." She pulls the things from her basket and chuckles loudly. "I have also brought some eggs to sell at the market tomorrow."

"Mama," I shout, "can I go to the market with Anita?"

Mama smiles, "We will all go, Kata. I have some shopping to do also."

The morning air is still crisp when we set out for the market. We walk at a slow pace so that Anita and Mama can keep up. Pablito and I peek into each shop window as we pass.

The market is busy with stands filled with people selling corn, eggs, tacos and many things that grow on small ranchitos. Carts, wagons, horses, burros and trucks are almost as numerous as the people that mill around buying and selling.

I grab on tightly to Anita's skirt for fear that I will lose her in the crowd. Mama carries Pablito so that he will not be hurt by the many bags that people carry.

Anita points to the water fountain that is in the center of the plaza. "We'll find a spot there under the tree."

We push and pull our way over to the tree. Once there, the people make room for us as they greet Anita happily. "Good to see you, Doña Anita. Sit here next to me," says a woman who holds a baby nursing at her breast.

"Many thanks, Doña Marta. How is the little one?" questions Anita as she lays out her blanket and eggs. "Kata, I birthed that baby. It was a fine birth, too," chuckles Anita. "I wish you could have been there."

"He's a pretty baby, Anita," I say, wishing I had been there, too.

A man passes with candy-coated apples. Anita whistles for his attention and then calls him over. "Give me two apples for the children." From her skirt pocket she pulls out her coin purse and pays the man. She hands me an apple, then one to Pablito.

"I have never seen such sticky red apples," I say as I kiss Anita on the cheek.

We sit there eating our apples while Anita sells her eggs. Mama leaves to look for things she needs. By lunch time, Anita has sold all her eggs and she pulls out her purse and puts all her coins in it. Then she rises saying, "I will go find your mother. Stay here with Doña Marta until I return."

"Yes, Anita," I say.

Soon they return, loaded with flour tortillas filled with minced barbecue meat. As we eat we sit and watch the men and women of the town tending to their business. I watch Mama, too, as she scans the crowds searching for Papa. Each time a tall man with a mustache walks by, she stiffens and rises to her knees to get a better glimpse. A heavy sigh escapes her lips and she sits down again to finish her lunch.

I leave with Mama to buy some fabric. I hold tightly to her hand as she leads me through the rows of stands. Finally we arrive at the right stand and she begins checking through the bolts of fabric, searching for the right color and price. "Kata, we need to make you a new skirt. Come help me pick the color."

All the colors and bolts of fabric soon confuse me, so I look out into the crowd. I see a tall slender man with a thick mustache hurrying by. I follow him, hoping he might be Papa. He stops at several stands down the row. "Papa!" I shout, but when he turns it is not my Papa.

"Kata!" yells Mama. "Katarina! Where are you?"

I turn and hurry back to the fabric stand.

"Kata, don't leave like that, you might get lost," scolds Mama.

"I just thought I saw Papa, but it wasn't him."

She puts down the bolt and looks at me. "I know how you feel child, but stay close to me. I'd hate to lose you, too."

"Yes, Mama," I answer, looking up into the faces of each tall man that passes.

That afternoon we are walking back to our room, seeking shelter from the scorching sun. Anita and I walk ahead, holding hands. Mama and Pablito follow at a snail's pace.

"This has been a very good day!" I declare.

Anita smiles, then answers, "Well, I wish you many more such good days."

"Anita, there are still many things I wish to do and to see. Most of all, I want Papa to come back. I want to learn how to read and write and how to sing!"

"My! What a long list!"

"There's more ... like being a healer like you. Perhaps a nurse or maybe a teacher. Would you like that?"

"Yes, but I'm afraid those wishes will take a little doing. Yet, with lots of patience and determination, who knows what can happen." She reaches over and pinches my cheek.

"Anita, do you think that they are all dreams like Papa's?"

"Kata, any thing is possible if one so wills it. But, you are the one that will have to work hard at it."

"Yes, it is so. I have lots to learn about this strange land." I take her hand. "Sometimes I forget that I'm no longer in Mexico."

Anita chuckles, "That's very easy to do in this little town with its plaza and market which are so much like the ones in Mexico. You see, the people here are mostly Mexicans, but they are born on this side of the river and that makes them Mexican-Americans. You were born on the other side of the river and that makes you a native Mexican.

"But Anita," I argue, "everyone speaks Spanish."

"Language has nothing to do with it. There is a government that runs Mexico and there is a different government that runs the United States." Anita chuckles on seeing me frown. "But, you will learn all about that in school."

"And when shall that be, Anita?"

She shrugs, "That I cannot say."

"In my old village we have to pay money to go to school."

"Yes, I know that is so, but here school is free."

"How lucky for the children," I add.

"Still, in this country there are many children that do not attend school."

"I would gladly go, Anita, even if I had to walk miles."

"Yes, I know you would. Look, we are almost home."

We flop down on the steps to wait for Mama and Pablito to catch up. It feels good to sit in the shade, relieved of all our packages. Anita sits with her eyes closed, and I watch the wrinkled circles around her eyes wiggle like when a rock is thrown into a pond. Her nose moves back and forth like a rabbit's.

I hear boots stomp at the top of the stairs. I look up to see the tattoed man staring down upon me. I wince as I feel the evil from those eyes enter my body as chills crawl up my scalp. I throw myself against Anita, who has awakened. She stands quickly and stares up at the man. A hissing sound grows on her lips as she points her clawed fingers at him. He rapidly disappears into one of the rooms upstairs.

Mama finds us wrapped around each other and staring at the top of the stairs. "What goes on here?" she asks.

"Perhaps it is best if you move from this place," warns Anita.

"But why?" she asks.

"As long as I am with you, you are safe, but I will worry for your safety when I leave."

Mama pulls me to her. "What has happened, Anita?"

"That man is after something. It is twice that he makes his evil appearances and three times he has tried to approach the girl."

"But we have nothing of value," adds Mama, stroking my hair.

"People value different things. He might want to hurt you or the child . . . as men sometimes do."

We make our way upstairs slowly while Anita talks to Mama in hushed tones, as if they were sharing deep secrets. By the time we reach our room, Mama is shaking. "Yes . . . yes . . . we must move immediately."

"Let me take the children back to the ranchito. Don Juan will arrive Sunday afternoon to drive me back. I can take the little ones until you are re-settled," Anita begs.

Mama sobs, "Oh, Anita. What else will happen to my little family?"

"Ah! You are fortunate so far. You have work, and I can care for the children. Don Juan likes the money you give him to drive you to and from the ranchito, so it works out well for everyone. Be thankful for that!"

"You speak the truth, Anita," replies Mama. "And I believe you are right." She turns to us. "Children, you rest now. Anita will stay with you while I go to speak with my lady boss. Perhaps she will know of a safer place to live. If not, I will send you back to the ranchito with Anita."

"Okay, Mama," I answer.

She dries her tears on the hem of her skirt, then hugs Anita. "Keep them safe until I return."

Anita locks the door after Mama leaves. "Rest now, a little sleep never hurt anyone."

I lie down next to Pablito. Anita covers us with a sheet and she sits on the mattress, humming a tune until I can no longer hear it. When I awake I notice Anita standing, glaring out the window. The sky is now dark. "Hasn't Mama returned?" I ask.

She seems startled by my voice. "No, come, for we must fix something for supper. It will help pass the time."

Anita connects the hot plate to the only electrical plug in our wall. She kneels on the floor, kneading dough for flour tortillas. Then she reaches over to test the hot plate with her finger.

"What time do you think it is?" I ask.

"It's late enough. Now come, for the baby will be hungry."

She hands me a bowl with the dough and I divide it into small balls, then roll them into flat circles. I hand them over to Anita who puts them on the hot plate. "If you are busy, time passes quickly," she mutters.

We roll a fine stack of tortillas which Anita wraps in a cloth and sticks in a basket. "Now, I will cook some meat."

I watch as she drops chopped meat into a pan to cook. She covers the pan with the lid and sits back to wait. When the meat is done, she fills each tortilla with a little meat and adds each taco to a neat stack. "Now, another cloth to keep them warm for Mama," she smiles.

She stops wrapping them when she hears a big thump, as if something heavy has fallen on the stairs. I glance quickly toward the door. "What is that?"

Again there is a heavy bang, as if something is thrown against the wall. This time Anita points to the floor beneath us. "It comes from down there." She rises to her feet and stares at the door.

"What's wrong?" I ask, rising too.

"Stay here. Lock the door after me."

I grab tightly to her skirt. "Don't leave us, Anita. Please."

"Be calm child. Now listen, I shall knock four times when I return. Do not let anyone else inside. Do you understand, Kata?"

"If you say so, Anita," I cry. She flies out the door and in the hall she waits until I have bolted the door, which I lean against with all my weight. It is as if the skin on my back is covered with biting black ants.

Chapter Six

The shadows from our small light seem to enlarge the room into a haunted house. My own shadow looms tall and thin before me, and the baby's shadow seems overgrown like a stuffed toad. I hurry to pick him up, and as I do he senses my fear and hugs me tightly. I wait, watching the glowing orange light of the hot plate turn bright brisk red. Loud slams and thuds add to my fears. It seems as though the bottom of the floor is tearing away and the walls shake from under the strain.

I want to unbolt the door and run out to the safety of the street, but I remember the strange man, and I remember what Anita bid me to do. Instead, I run to the mattress, grab Pablito and bury my face in the mattress until the floor stops shaking and all is still.

Four loud knocks break the silence. I jump up and unbolt the door to find Anita standing with the sleeve of her dress torn and a long scratch from her eye to her chin, which bleeds onto her breasts. Anita carries Mama in her arms. She is limp as a doll. I stand speechless, unable to move as Anita carries her to the mattress and lays her down gently.

"Mama! Anita! What has happened?" I cry as I bolt the door.

"Hush!" hisses Anita as her eyes show a fearsome wild rage.

The front of Mama's blouse is ripped apart, as is her skirt. Her legs are bruised with deep patches of purple and red running along the inside. Deep welts along her arms lead to a bruise the size of my fist upon her cheek. Blood trickles from her mouth and onto her neck.

"That man . . . he . . . we must get help for her," mutters Anita. Without warning, she collapses onto the mattress beside Mama. I can see that they are both hurt badly and that I must get help for them. I dash to the door, but before I reach it there is a sharp splattering of wood. An arm bursts through as if it were a steel hammer crushing the wood into a million splinters.

I feel a scream swelling in my throat. I stand frozen as a hairy arm with a tattooed lady reaches for the knob and turns it. I rush back to Pablito and drag him to the darkest corner. The door swings open as if it were made of cardboard.

The man approaches the mattress where Anita and Mama lay helpless. He moves slowly as if in a daze, then stares down at them for a long time, unaware that we are huddled in the corner behind him.

My body urges me to get out of the room as quickly as I can, so I start creeping toward the door holding Pablito tightly. The baby cries out in objection to my tight grip. I rush toward the door, but a strong force drags me back. I pull against it, realizing that he must have caught my skirt.

I scream and turn back to see Anita tackling him around his knees. She bites into his leg and he turns to kick her, and I struggle loose and escape, running down the stairs unaware of Pablito's weight.

I run into the street yelling for help. Two men see me and pass me as if I were a dirty begger. Other people only stare and walk around me. I keep screaming for help at the top of my lungs until at last a man and a woman stop. They calm me and the baby down long enough for me to explain what has happened. Soon, other men join them, and I point to the room, and they follow me up the stairs like a crowd at a bull fight.

As we enter the room someone screams and a man yells. The tattooed man bolts out from behind the remains of the door.

"That's him!" I scream.

The tattooed man and another man start fighting and they fall against the wall, knocking a woman over Mama. The woman yells out and her man friend jumps onto the tattooed man, who flips in the air and lands on top of Anita. He rolls off quickly and dives toward the door under rows of legs.

Once outside the door, he meets more men and pushes them out of his way. "Stop that crazy man!" screams the woman at the top of her lungs.

The men gang up on him, kicking and shoving him around until soon I hear a piercing scream followed by a loud thud, then nothing but silence.

Finally a man says, "He's dead. He broke his neck when he fell down the stairs."

"He deserves it!" snaps another.

"Woman beater!" shouts the woman loudly. "He needed to die!"

This seems to me like a dream, but I know it is not. For Mama still lays on the mattress and Anita lies in the corner where she has been shoved. She bleeds heavily from her mouth. A policeman plows through the growing crowd of people and he is followed by more police, who arrive and begin to clear the room of the lingering crowd.

A man in a dark suit arrives and gives orders freely. I watch as he snaps open a black bag and then I realize that he is a doctor. "Doña Anita," he says, "what have you gotten yourself into this time?" He kneels in front of her.

"Anita saved us!" I yell.

"So, she has done another miracle, but this time she will have to pay a bit more for her work." He holds a small bottle to her nose.

Anita struggles with him, but when she hears his quiet commands, she settles back and accepts his aid.

"Anita, we are fine," I add, hoping to cheer her. She raises her hand in response and then goes limp.

The doctor finishes her bandages and leaves her lying there. "We shall let her sleep this one out. It would be best." He rises and goes over to Mama.

I follow him and watch closely as he looks into her eyes, then down her mouth. Next he feels her ribs and it is then that he notices the small bandaid on her side. "Ah . . . this looks like the work of Doña Anita." He removes the bandaid with a quick jerk, then looks up at me. "Is this not so?"

I nod and he returns to his work.

"Who is this woman?"

"My Mama."

"I see. Well, I will have to take them both to the hospital. The ambulance is waiting outside. Come with me, little girl, and bring the boy."

We wait near the door while men in white arrive carrying stretchers. They carry Mama out first, then return for Anita. I clutch Pablito's hand. I do not know what to do, for everyone seems to be getting into cars and slamming doors.

The doctor turns back to us. "You and the boy will have to go with Officer Gonzalez. I shall come see you later."

A strong hand touches my shoulder and leads me to a police car. Gonzalez puts us in the back seat and slams and locks the door. He goes to the front of the car and starts the engine. He is about to pull out onto the street when the doctor's face appears outside the window.

"These policemen will not take us to jail will they?" I ask as I roll down the car window.

"No, just to a place where you can rest and wait for me to return."

"Please help Mama and Anita."

"I will," he says.

I watch him enter the ambulance and close the door. As it speeds off, I cry on Pablito's shoulder, but he wiggles away from me and pulls off the officer's hat. If this is the greatest of all lands, why is everyone I love getting hurt? It is not so easy in this new land. I prefer the quiet life of the old village and the ranchito to all this confusion.

The police car speeds onward, tossing us around as if we were balls and, in time, it comes to a screeching halt. I peek out the window and ask, "What is this place?"

"The Youth Center," the officer replies.

"I don't like it!" I protest on seeing black bars on the windows.

The officer lifts Pablito to his chest. Immediately Pablito pulls on his black mustache, which makes the officer laugh. He takes my hand and leads us into the faded brick building. "I'm sorry you don't like it here, niña, but for right now it's the best we can do."

We walk into a small yellow room where there is a desk in the center and on one of the walls there is a picture of a red-haired clown.

"Nell! Are you here?" he shouts. His voice echoes and bounces off the walls. He waits impatiently and when he does not receive an answer, he turns and peeks down the hall. "Wait here, I'll be back."

I climb into a chair and pull Pablito onto the next one. Soon I hear voices, one happy and the other muttering in hushed tones. I figure it is the officer returning with the woman he calls Nell.

She smiles as she enters the room. I stare at her, and I cannot help doing so, for if God makes angels, this is one that he sent to earth. She is beautiful, like nothing I have ever seen before.

"Hello, there. Such darlings!"

We respond with unknowing stares. So she looks up toward Officer Gonzalez.

He chuckles, "You have to speak Spanish, Nell. They don't understand English."

"I should have known." She bends down on her knees and looks us straight in the eyes. "Are you hungry?" she asks with spoon to mouth gestures.

The baby grabs her long blond hair in his hand and pulls at it playfully. She does not attempt to remove Pablito's hand, but lets him handle it. I ache to touch those golden strands for I have never seen such a fair person with eyes that are grey-blue, the color of the angry sky just before a storm breaks.

She laughs as Pablito pulls hard. Without realizing it, I reach out to touch her hair. She immediately takes my hand in hers and I bow my head in shame, then notice her hands.

"Señora, what fine fingernails."

"Gracias, niña, perhaps after we eat I can paint yours."

I pull my hand away embarrassed, because I feel dirty standing next to such a nice creature who does not mind taking my sticky hand. I hang my head in shame, like an ostrich ploughs his head into the dirt.

"If you like, we can have a bath, too." She touches my nose with her long slender finger. "What do you think about that idea?" She doesn't wait for my answer. She turns, "Officer Gonzalez, the children are in my care. Continue with your duties."

"Be nice to Nell, children." He nods and turns down the hall.

She lifts the baby to her arms and then takes my hand. We enter a corridor which leads to a room that is painted a faint blue, like the sky after a fresh rainfall. There are four little beds in that room which are surrounded by shelves that are loaded with books and toys. In the center of the room is a table with chairs painted to match the walls. Pablito lets out a shout of joy as he sees all the colorful toys. Immediately he makes his way over to them.

"Ramona, please come here." Nell stands near a door painted white. She smiles back at me encouragingly. A woman appears who is middle-aged, dark skinned and does not smile when we are presented. Nell, I notice, is not shy about giving orders, nor does the woman jump to do what she is asked.

"Ramona, bathe the girl, then get her some clean clothes," commands Nell.

The woman holds out her hand, signaling me to follow her, but I hesitate, then look at Nell and say, "You come with me, señora Nell."

"Why, darling, I have to watch the baby while you bathe. Go on with Ramona and I'll come check on you later." She touches my shoulder. "Ramona will not harm you and I'll be right here in this room."

We enter a very tiny room filled with a huge white bath tub that seems as cold as can be. I watch as Ramona bends on her knees and twists two knobs that are clear like glass. Water rushes out of them at great speed. I gasp. I reach out to touch the water with my finger. It is cold. Ramona pulls a large bottle down from a shelf. She unscrews the cap and pours the pink liquid into the water. Soon, huge white bubbles appear covering the water completely.

Ramona turns and pulls at my blouse. I struggle with her. "No! I can undress myself!" I shout.

She frowns, then twists the glass knobs, and the water stops. Then she rises and leaves the room. I stand alone for a few seconds, then touch the bath tub with all my hand. It is very cold. I reach in and touch the bubbles and water. They are nice and warm.

I untie the pouch and look around for a safe place to hide it. I see that the bath tub has clawed feet, so I feel behind them and find that they are hollow. I roll the pouch into a tight ball and push it into one of the claws, then I finish undressing and slip into the white foaming water that Ramona has prepared.

Ramona returns. I study her face as she picks up my dirty clothes with the tip of her fingers. Her face seems made of stone. She says not a word, but from the expression on her face she does not need words. I stick my tongue out at her as she leaves the room. Then I cross my fingers because she has not looked down at the spot where I hid the pouch.

The white bubbles glue themselves to my body, tickling me and then bursting into little rainbows of color. The more I move in the water, the higher the mountains of bubbles become. This is a fun bath, I decide. Back in the old village we took our baths in the stream, but we never had this much fun because the water was always too cold or too muddy to linger in it.

Nell enters the room with Pablito. "How are you doing, Kata?" Pablito stares at the bubbles, then screams. Quickly he escapes Nell and sticks his hand into the water. Nell pulls him back, "No, it's not your turn, yet."

I laugh because Pablito's arm is covered with suds. He smears them across Nell's face, but she is not angry. She laughs as she wipes the suds off her face and off his arms.

Ramona enters and Nell leaves with Pablito. The silent one washes my hair, scrubbing until my head feels like it will fall off. I watch with bowed head as the dirt from my hair seems to kill the beautiful bubbles.

"This will fit her." Nell bursts in the room carrying a dress that is green and gold, the colors of green peppers and squash. She stands watching as Ramona slips the dress over my shoulders.

"I declare! You look mighty different!" Nell circles me for a better view. "And your hair is just like coal with gold strands peeking through. Everything's perfect!"

The silent one only nods, still refusing to smile. Suddenly, a big splash of water soaks the front of my dress. Nell screams and Ramona jumps into action. Pablito has managed to fall into the tub full of water. With one big thrust, Ramona puts in her arm and yanks him up. He opens his eyes wide, looking very frightened, but then he starts laughing.

"Pablito! You are very bad!" snaps Nell with her hand over her heart. "Ramona, bathe him while I feed Kata." She takes a towel and dries my skirt, then leads me into the other room.

My dinner waits on a tray. I do not like my first taste of American food. The meat needs chile and I do not like the green stringy stuff. I wonder what has happened to the basket of tortillas that Anita and I rolled.

Nell sits across from me talking in her broken Spanish. "The doctor will be here in the morning. He will want to speak with you. Do you understand what I am saying?" Her eyes search mine.

I nod that I understand, but I ask, "Will Pablito stay here with me?" This time I search her face to see if she understands me.

She looks a little puzzled, then a big smile breaks over her face. "Yes, so will Ramona." She rises and squeezes my shoulder. "We'll do all right, niña. Now, I have to go home, but I will see you first thing in the morning."

I nod. "Si, señora."

Nell turns. "Señorita Nell. You see, Kata, I'm not married."

"You are too beautiful not to be married," I say.

"Thank you. You won't be afraid here, will you? You have been so good." I nod that I wouldn't and she adds, "Remember, you are safe here."

The silent one enters carrying Pablito. He shines like silver rinsed in the stream. I have never seen him so clean. She has dressed him in a blue and yellow shirt and has put a soft white paper on his bottom. "What is that?" I ask touching the paper.

"It's a Pamper. It's like a paper diaper. After he dirties it, I throw it away. No washing needed."

"It doesn't hurt him?" I ask.

"No."

Pablito yawns and rubs his eye, seeking sleep.

"I'm leaving now, Ramona. Take care of the children," Nell orders as she closes the door. "I will be here early tomorrow morning. So will the doctor." She waves goodbye to me and slowly closes the door.

"May I play with Pablito a little while?" I ask.

Ramona brings him over and places him on the bed with me. We look through a picture book together while the silent one pulls down the covers on the bed.

"Are you ready to sleep?" she asks in a low man-like voice.

"Yes," I answer.

She comes for Pablito and puts him in the bed with the wooden bars. She covers him and stands watching until he falls asleep, then she comes to check my blanket.

"Do you have children?" I ask.

"No." Then she turns out the light.

I toss, turn and count my fingers while sleep takes its time in coming. I finally doze off, but I feel like I am suffocating in a hot thick grey mist. I sweat, but I soon become frightened as the mist burns my hair and skin. The more I struggle to get out of the mist, the thicker it becomes. At last it engulfs me in a long endless tunnel.

"Mama!" I scream.

I awake trembling like an earthquake. Ramona immediately seizes me and she strokes my hair until I fall back into a calm sleep. With her hands she pushes away the mist, the tattooed arm, the blood on Anita's face and the bruises on Mama.

My eyelids open slowly like a butterfly on its first early morning flight. Pablito is spread-eagle, laying on his stomach. My eyes float down to where Ramona sleeps. Her mild snores add music to the early twilight.

I need to go to the outhouse . . . a bathroom . . . as the white ones call it. I ease myself into a sitting position, then lower my feet to the floor. I stand watching the silent one for any signs of waking.

Step by step, like a slow moving turtle, I make my way over to the door. I push it open only enough for me to slip through, then I glance back. No one has moved, and the snores have not stopped their up and down rhythm.

I touch the tub which is even colder than the night before. I reach for the pouch, find it, untangle it, then tie it under the white cotton slip they have given me. I smooth down the slip, then study the white hole with its swirling water. I dread sitting on it because I know it is cold, but I must go, so I quickly use it, and then push the little handle down. Quickly I stand so that I can watch the water in the hole swirl faster, then disappear.

It's magic, I think, watching the hole refill itself. On going back into the blue room, I notice the silent one has hardly moved. I crawl back into bed smiling to myself. With my treasure safe around my waist, I fall asleep again.

I awake with a start when I hear a man's voice outside the door. I recognize it as the doctor's. I glance over to Ramona's bed, but it is made and she is gone. I sit up quickly and notice that Pablito is still sleeping.

Nell enters. "Well, it's about time, young lady. Did you have a good night's rest?"

I tighten the blanket around me and watch as she goes over to Pablito. "He's still sleeping," she says as she feels his forehead. Satisfied he is all right, she turns to me and says, "Doctor Mendez is waiting for you." She hands me my dress from the chair and watches as I slip out of the blanket and pull the dress over my head. "I think it would be best if you speak with him before having breakfast. he is a very busy man." She brushes my hair quickly. "We would not want to keep him from his work.

"Yes, he needs to get back to Anita and Mama."

Nell chuckles, "Kata, there are other sick people

besides your Mama and Anita." She holds the door
open for me.

"Yes, señorita Nell."

She leads me to the small office where the doctor
waits. He looks like he has not slept all night long.
"Chiquita, little one, let's talk." He points to a chair. I
wait while he clears his throat.

"Anita is doing much better now, even though she
lost several teeth. Her face is swollen, but it will heal
in a few days. Her ribs are very bruised, but the X-
rays show nothing broken."

"What about Mama?" I interrupt.

"She is not much better today. She has many broken ribs which will take time to heal." He clears his
throat again and glances around the office for some
water. Finding none, he continues, "She does not
wake up and we need you to come see her so that she
will want to wake up and speak."

"I will come right now," I declare.

"Ah, perhaps a little later, but I feel your talking
with her might help her along."

"Doctor," I interrupt, "can I see Anita too?"

"Yes, of course. Nell will drive you over later this
afternoon." He turns to pick up his bag. "Also, the
police want to speak with you."

"Police!" I rise quickly and say, "Oh, no! Can't
they wait until I see Mama?"

"If you like," he answers, surprised at my outburst.

"I have to see Mama first, then Anita, and then
the police."

"That's fine, I will arrange it."

I bow to him. "Thanks to you, good doctor."

He touches the top of my head, then leaves the
office in a big hurry. I go to the door and look after

him as he walks down the hall. Nell happens to come out of a side door, and the doctor slows his pace, tips his hat, then speeds onward.

Nell stares after him for a moment, stands looking down at her hands for such a long time, and then she shakes her long hair and smiles sadly. The doctor stops at the front door and slowly turns back. Their eyes meet for a second, and it is Nell who turns her back and walks off.

Chapter Seven

I stand in the hospital room looking down at Mama. Lying under the sheet so still, she's never seemed so tall to me. I reach out and take her hand. "Mama, it's me, Kata."

I peer into her eyes, but they remain closed. "Mama, wake up please." I touch her chin and turn her head towards me. "Mama, speak to me. Tell me what to do with the pouch."

I stroke her hand gently, remembering that she was never this hard to wake, not even in the middle of the night. "Mama, the police want to talk to me. Shall I tell them about Papa?" I touch her shoulder and shake her gently. "Mama, please wake up!" I crawl onto the edge of the bed. "What am I to do?" I sob.

After several moments of getting no answer, I turn towards the door. I can see Nell waiting down the hall. I kiss Mama's cheek, then join Nell who says, "She isn't well, is she?"

"No, I hope Anita is better." We walk down the hall to Anita's room. I take a deep breath before I push open the door.

"Would you like me to go inside with you?" asks Nell.

I hesitate then glance up. "No, I'd better go myself."

Anita turns my way as I enter the room "Kata!"

I rush to her and bury my head in her arm. "Anita!" I sob.

Her voice is soft. "Don't worry, Kata. God will take care of us. You will see."

"But you are both so sick. What am I to do? Mama cannot speak or see." I seize her hand. "Anita,"

I whisper, "the police are going to ask me questions. What shall I tell them?"

"I have already spoken with them. Just tell them you are my adopted grandchild."

"But, what if they ask about Papa?"

"I do not think they will ask about him. All they want to know is what you saw happen the night your Mama and I got hurt."

"I am still scared. What if they decide to take Pablito from us."

"They can't do that. Don't worry, all will be well. Have faith, little one." She strokes my hair, then seems to fall into a light sleep. I stay with her a while, then go out to the hall.

"How did it go?" asks Nell.

"She fell asleep."

"She needs rest. Come, I'll go with you to see the sergeant."

"You will!"

"Of course. Didn't Doctor Mendez tell you I would?"

"No, but he was in a big hurry."

"Doctors are always in a hurry, Kata."

"Anita is like a doctor. I mean, she can fix people up, but she's never in a hurry."

"Oh, is that how Anita works? I don't see how you can compare the old woman to a doctor," adds Nell, as if she has just broken a rotten egg.

As Nell circles the station looking for a parking space, I wonder if I will see Officer Gonzalez again. There are so many men dressed in the same uniform that I know I will never be able to recognize him.

After we park, Nell takes my hand and rushes me past one office after another. Finally, we enter one and Nell goes right up to the desk. Sergeant Estrada, this is Katarina Campos. We understand that you want to see her," declares Nell in a business-like voice.

"Yes, I've been waiting." He rises from his chair.

I feel myself freeze up, but I say nothing. I watch Nell take a seat in front of his desk and motion for me to sit next to her.

The sergeant continues, "Tell me about this man that hurt your Mama and Anita Morales."

"I can't remember much except that tattoo on his arm."

"Where did you meet him?"

"I didn't. I saw him in a dream and then at the apartment house."

He stops writing to look up at me, then at Nell. "A dream, you say."

I nod. "In the dream I woke up before I saw Anita and Mama got hurt."

"Did he live at the apartment house?" He taps his pencil against the desk.

"I don't know."

I watch as he bites his lips, "He's dead, you know."

I nod. "Yes, I heard them shout that he broke his neck when he fell down the stairs." I wiggle in my chair. "Who was he?" I ask.

"That's my question!" he snaps. "Are you sure that your Mama didn't know him?"

I shrug. "We just came from Anita's ranchito."

"Yes, I know. Doña Anita explained all that." He writes something on his pad. "Are you her grand-child?"

He waits for my answer, but I give none. Instead, I cough a long time, then Nell slaps my back.

The sergeant stares at me a long while, then says, "That man probably crossed the border illegally. Perhaps he's a wetback who doesn't have papers or identification. We get men like that here all the time."

"Well, he deserved to die because he hurt Mama and Anita," I snap back at him, then begin to tremble. I grip the chair tightly, glancing back at Nell. My heart races at the sound of the word "papers."

"Okay, that will be all for now," he says.

Nell rises. "Thank you, sergeant. If you need us we will be at the center."

"I know where I can find you, Miss Nell. Keep her around so that if I need her, I can get hold of her quickly."

Nell nods and takes my hand. "Until her mother is well and able, the girl will be housed at the center."

Once out in the hall I ask, "Is it true that we'll be staying at the center until Mama gets well?"

Nell smiles. "It's the best I can do for right now."

"That's great!" I cry.

"Why, Kata?"

"Because I like you and I even like Ramona, whom I have named the silent one."

"Why do you call her that?" Nell holds open the car door.

"Because she hardly speaks."

"You are a silly girl, Kata. Ramona is a silent one and you've made Anita a doctor. What shall you think of next?"

I shrug, "But that's how I see them!"

Pablito acts like a happy puppy when we arrive from the Police Station. He quickly crawls over and hands me a toy. Nell leaves to speak with Ramona, who is in the kitchen. I feel it is safe to pull out the pouch and examine it again.

The stone, which is as heavy and as big as my large toe, falls out into my palm. I turn it around in my fingers and go over to the window and hold it up to the sunlight. Where did it come from, I wonder?

The gold sparkle has caught Pablito's eye and he tries to pull my arm down so that he can play with it. "No, Pablito, this is special! I know it is or else Mama would not have saved it for so long." I replace the stone into the pouch and retie it around my waist. Pablito watches me with wonder, then touches his own waist.

Nell enters the room. "Well, children, Ramona will have dinner ready in a few minutes. Why don't we go wash our hands."

Pablito crawls beside me and pokes his little hand up my skirt. Unable to reach my waist, he tugs at my dress and slip, almost pulling them off. "No! Pablito!" I command.

"What is it? What does he want?" asks Nell.

"Oh, he just wants me to carry him." I bend down and pick him up, then take him to the bathroom. After we scrub our hands and seat ourselves at the table, Ramona bursts into the room pushing a cart.

"Oh!" I gasp standing up quickly. "What is it?"

"We call it a cake, Kata."

"It's fantastico!"

"I believe it is," answers Nell.

Pablito has both hands outstretched reaching for the cake, but the highchair holds him firmly planted in his seat. He wiggles and squirms, trying to get out so that he can get a handful of cake.

"Look, Pablito!" I poke his fingers into the frosting. "Cake," I say repeating Nell's word. I laugh as he licks his fingers and smiles.

"But children, we must eat all our supper before we get to eat the cake," demands Nell in a gentle voice.

"Okay, señorita Nell, if you say we must."

Nell helps Ramona serve our plates. She laughs as Pablito opens his mouth wide for bite after bite, never once taking his eyes off the cake. I believe he understands every word Nell said. Occasionally he reaches for the cake and cries out, but Nell puts another spoonful of potatoes into his mouth.

I am anxious myself, for I have never tasted an American cake, which seems very different from our Mexican pastries. This cake seems to melt before my eyes, and I know it has to be delicious.

After Nell is satisfied that we have eaten all the food she can manage to get into our stomachs, she starts cutting the cake into very large pieces. She purposely cuts it slow and then licks her fingers before our eyes. As soon as she hands Pablito his slice, he jams his fingers into it and pushes piece after piece into his mouth, chewing like a happy calf and smearing chocolate from his nose to his belly.

After my first bite, I put the spoon down and use my fingers. The cake is creamy, messy and the best thing I have ever tasted in my life. Would Mama like this cake, I wonder? I know she would.

My two slices disappear quickly, and I ask for a third, but Nell refuses. Upon seeing my disappointment she says, "You'll get some more tomorrow. You wouldn't want to get a sick tummy, would you?"

"I would not mind a sick stomach!" I argue, but she remains firm.

"No, Kata. Tomorrow is another day."

What could I tell her? Tomorrow is far away and that delicious cake sits before me. Tomorrow brings who knows what, and I might never get to taste the cake again, but Nell stands between me and that cake, like the hospital separates me from Mama.

"Please, Nell," I beg.

"Sorry, Kata, but I'm the boss here." With her hand she motions for Ramona to take the cake away.

I have learned much in this land called Texas, but nothing as wonderful as that chocolate cake that Ramona baked.

Three days later Nell bursts into my room. "Kata, the doctor is here, and he waits to speak with you in my office. So, hurry, child."

I put down the toys and turn to follow her to the room she calls "office." She enters first and pulls a chair out for me to sit upon. I sit and watch the doctor speaking quietly into a black horn that Nell calls her telephone. He has his back turned to us, but pivots when he hears Nell close the door as she leaves.

He slowly puts the horn into its box, then smiles at me. "Good morning, Kata. I have a surprise for you." He points to another door.

"Anita!" I shout as I throw myself into her fat arms. "You are well and here!"

She laughs, "Yes, I am well and stand before you. It does not take old Anita long to recover from an illness." She peers over at the doctor with her snapping good eye. "I would have recovered sooner had I had some of my own medicine."

The doctor stiffens and says, "We study two distinct arts that accomplish the same healing goal, Doña Anita."

Anita refuses to answer, but glares at him as if he has just slugged her with a hammer. She grunts as she swings into the nearest chair.

Doctor Mendez turns to me and says, "Your mother is better, but still refuses to speak. She will have to remain in the hospital another week or so."

"Humph," grunts Anita. "If she had my herbal tea she would already be walking around!"

The doctor bites his lips and says, "Please, Doña Anita. May I remind you that this is my consultation with Kata." He continues, "Your mother has broken ribs which will have to heal before we move her." He glances over at Anita,expecting her to say more, but she remains silent. "Therefore, we have a little problem that we must attempt to solve." He looks directly at me. "Anita would like to go home to her ranchito."

"And," adds Anita quickly, "I would like you and Pablito to come with me." She takes my hand in hers.

"Or," interrupts the doctor, "you may stay with Nell here at this center until your mother is well. But, I must warn you that it may not be for some time to come, or it could be only a day or so."

"Well, Kata. The decision is yours," says Anita.

Both of them say nothing more, and the silence that follows is frightening. It is expected of me to make a decision between going home with Anita to the ranchito and not seeing Mama, or staying here and not seeing Anita.

I turn to Anita. "Mama needs me more, but I need you, too. What shall I do, Anita?"

"Ah, it's hard to make up your mind, but you must do it yourself. I cannot do it for you," she answers.

I chew on my fingers and glance from face to face, seeking the answer. Doctor Mendez smiles and Anita pats my hand, but they both wait.

After seeing that I cannot decide, Doctor Mendez rises and speaks, "I have a suggestion. You might not care for it, but on the other hand, you might."

"Well, speak your mind man!" orders Anita in a huff.

"Si, señora. What if Pablito goes home with Anita, so that she may look after him. After all, he's still a baby, and Kata stays here with Nell so that she may visit her Mama each day, in that way speeding her recovery?"

I will miss Pablito, but if he is safe with Anita, I will have less to worry about and I can see Mama every day. Yes, I like the idea, but I still turn to Anita for a clue as to how she feels about it. "Anita, what do you think?"

"Well, it sounds good, but only if you like it. Your Mama has to come back to the ranchito to recover fully, then we will all be together."

"It is settled," I say. "I shall stay with Nell and Pablito will go with you." I lean over and whisper to her, "Anyway, Papa might be there."

"Perhaps so," answers Anita. She turns to the doctor. "Sir, do you feel the child will be safe here for so much time? I understand that Miss Nell has another charge now."

"She will be safe, Doña Anita. Let me assure you. If you want, I will personally see to it that she is entertained as much as possible."

Anita stomps her foot. "Her care is what I am concerned about, doctor, not her entertainment! I have heard many stories about this place."

Irritated, Doctor Mendez rises and walks to the front of the desk. "Anita, I assure you that she is safe here."

Anita quickly rises and stands face to face with him. "And, I tell you that she is not. Any man can walk right in here and do her harm!"

Doctor Mendez's jaw bulges out. "Would you feel better, Doña Anita, if she stays at my house?"

Much to his surprise, Anita answers, "Yes, I would feel much better, especially since there is a favor you owe me, if I do recall properly."

The doctor studies his hands for a moment. "Yes, I owe you, and I shall be happy to have Kata as a guest in my house. I shall call Pilar immediately."

Anita bows slightly, "Consider all debts paid."

"Anita and doctor," I interrupt, "please, do not fight because of me. It does not matter where I stay and, Anita, I do like Nell and I do like the center."

The doctor speaks first. "It is settled. Kata stays with me. Nell will drive her over this afternoon."

"When will you leave?" I ask Anita.

"Now, as soon as I can get Pablito. The doctor will have me driven home, since he is a good person." She winks at him and he immediately turns away.

I throw myself at her. "I'll miss you, old one."

She strokes my back gently. "Now, you must show me where they have the baby, so that we can be on our way."

I take her hand and lead her out of the office and into the hall where Nell waits. Her sparkling eyes deepen into a dark gusty grey. She doesn't like Anita. I can tell by the way she ignores her and forces her to walk behind her down the hall. I say nothing. Instead, I cling tighter to Anita's hand.

Pablito screams when he sees Anita and they smash against each other. She swings him into the air, kissing him and hugging him and he is happy. I am glad he is going with Anita, for they seem made for each other. I watch as Anita lets him slobber all over her face.

"Come on, little man. It's time for us to go home," chuckles Anita.

"Wait!" shouts Nell. "Ramona will want to say goodbye to him." She hurries out of the room.

Anita turns to me. "Talk to your mother as much as you can. Speak loudly in her ear and let her know your voice. She will come around, but it will take time. When I visit next, I will bring a special tea for her, and it will make her feel much better."

"I will remember what you say," I answer.

"Good girl."

"Anita, when are you coming again?"

"The following weekend. Once I am home, I will ask questions about your Papa. I have not heard a thing here in town."

Ramona enters the room. "Señora Morales, it is my pleasure, for I have heard of you and your miraculous cures for many years now." She takes Anita's hand and kisses it.

"I must thank you for taking care of the children. You will not go unrewarded in this life."

"There is no need for thanks," interrupts Ramona. "I have enjoyed them so."

"Well," stammers Nell. "Now that that is over with, we'd best be on our way." She goes to the door and holds it open for Anita and Pablito. I follow after them, then notice that Pablito carries a small wooden truck in his hand.

"Nell, he has the toy truck."

"Oh, let him keep it. A small gift from us."

Anita stops walking and says, "Thank you." Then she continues to the entrance, where a car is waiting at the door. Anita and Pablito climb into the back seat and turn to wave. The car speeds out of sight and I wave until my arm hurts.

"Kata, come inside," orders Nell.

I enter the building slowly. "Why don't you like Anita?"

Nell stops walking. "She is a very strange woman. She's very set in her old ways. You see, I really don't dislike her, it's just that I have a hard time accepting her for what she is and for what other's say of her."

"What do others say?"

"Oh, look, don't worry about it. You'll understand more when you get older."

I frown. "Mama says that all the time, but Anita would never say such a thing because she believes everyone has a right to know the answers to all questions."

"So, that's how your Anita thinks!" snaps Nell. "Well, don't go comparing me with Anita and don't expect me to believe in her either."

This is the first time I've seen Nell angry. She's not such an angel after all. She's just a pretty lady whose halo has fallen off.

Once inside the room, Nell turns and says, "Kata, I have to run an errand. I'll return later. Ramona is in the kitchen."

I sit on the bed and glance through a book. I already miss Anita and Pablito. My hand reaches to the pouch on my waist as if it were the only thing left from my previous life.

I remember that Doctor Mendez seems irritated with Anita at times, but the doctor respects Anita and her wishes. Nell seems to fear her magic and powers. Ramona, on the other hand, seems to worship the ground on which Anita walks.

I decide that Anita has a power with a deep kind of pull that enables her to make people act like puppets. All I know is that next to Mama and Papa, I love her the best. I must have fallen asleep because several hours later Nell wakes me up.

"I bought this for you." She opens a bag and pulls out a dress.

"Nell," I gasp, "it's beautiful."

"I thought you might look good in it."

"Thanks, Nell. I've never owned a dress before."

"It's a gift from me to say that I like you."

I finger the dress and bite my lips saying nothing.

Nell continues, "After all, you must look nice at the doctor's house."

"I like you, too," I whisper.

Chapter Eight

I watch as Ramona packs my clothes into a small plastic bag. She seems deep in thought, so I do not ask her questions. After she finishes packing, she reaches for the brush and sits on the edge of the bed. "Come here, let me fix your hair."

I stand between her knees with a bent head, wincing as she pulls the brush through my long hair. After she has brushed my hair for what seems like a hundred strokes, she fixes it into two long braids and ties each end with pink ribbons. Then she turns me around to smooth out my bangs. "You look nice," she says.

"Ramona, I do not want to leave here," I say as I lay my head against her shoulder. "I do not know those people."

"Katarina, you did not know us when you arrived and now you do. So, it will be easy enough for you to learn to know them."

"But, for how long will I have to stay with them?" I ask, refusing to accept the fact that once again I must leave the people I have come to like.

"I am sure Doña Anita would not have let you go there if they were not good people." She pats my shoulder. "You must trust Anita, for she is a very wise woman."

"You are right, silent one," I answer, pulling away from her and wiping my nose.

Suddenly Ramona starts laughing, "Why do you call me that?"

"Because you use few words and all that you feel shows in your face and eyes."

She crushes me against her chest. "Oh, Kata, how

I wish I had a little girl like you. Then, I would truly enjoy going home."

I sniffle. "Anita will help you, and I know you are going to make a nice mama for some little baby."

Her voice cracks as she answers, "I will never forget you, Kata." Then she buries her head in my shoulder.

I sit on my bed and study the walls full of toys and books, and I wonder who bought them all. Nell enters the room and smiles down at me. "Kata," she says, "I would like you to meet someone. This little girl is called Betty."

I watch as a little girl with golden curls slides from behind Nell. She seems not to notice me at all, for her eyes are very wide and she looks frightened, but she stares at all the toys that line the room.

Nell gets down on her knees. "Betty, this is Kata."

"How old is she?" I ask.

Nell leans over to the small table. "I believe she's about five or six. We don't know yet."

I walk over to Betty and stare down at her. "Why are you here?"

"She doesn't speak Spanish, Kata. She's lost and we cannot find her parents."

"She's very small and she looks very hungry."

"Yes, and she hasn't spoken two words since she's been here. But, she did say her name was Betty. Why don't you play with her while I go fix her a tray with something to eat."

I watch as Betty keeps her eyes glued to a small

doll. She seems frightened like a baby rabbit which is about to bolt away. I take the doll and put it in her arms, then touch her short golden curls which are like soft cotton fresh from the field.

Betty sobs then buries her face in the doll's dress and then she starts to cry. I step back, fearing that perhaps I have hurt her, but she continues to cry even harder. I retreat to my bed and sit there watching her. Then without warning, I, too, begin to cry.

After a long while Betty stops crying and I wonder if she is sleeping, for she does not move. I sit and watch her for fear she will fall out of the chair.

Ramona enters carrying a tray of food. "You have met the little one?"

"Yes. I feel sad for her. She cried for a long time."

Ramona nods. It is best that she has a good hard cry now, so that later she will feel better." She takes Betty in her arms and sits her on her lap. Betty seems like a limp doll and only takes the food because Ramona forces her to.

Nell comes into the room and stands watching Ramona feed Betty. She then turns to me and says, "Kata, we must go. Pilar will be expecting you by four this afternoon." She picks up my plastic bag, "Ramona, I will be back as soon as I drop off Kata."

Ramona nods, then looks up at me and smiles. "We shall meet again, Kata. Go with God."

"If it's God's will, Ramona." I take Nell's hand and leave the room.

The drive to the doctor's house is a short one. Nell drives fast around some curves, as if she is in a big hurry. I glance up at her face and see that she is sad. "Are you sad, Nell?"

"No, not sad, Kata. Just a littly angry and nervous. The house is around this block." She stops the

93

car. "This is the place, Kata. Shall we get out?"

I stretch to look out of the car window at a big two-story house that is white as ground flour. "Is this where the doctor lives?"

Nell takes her purse from the rear seat. "Yes."

"Doctor Mendez is very rich, no?"

"Not so rich, but well-to-do. You see, we have only three doctors in this town. So, he gets his share of patients and their money." Nell sighs. "Come on, let's get out. She'll be waiting inside." Her door slams and she goes around to open mine.

We stand searching the big house for a few moments. Looking up at Nell, I can see creases set deeply in her forehead and her eyes almost seem to draw into a small line. She bites her lips as is she does not want to go inside the house.

"Is something wrong, Nell?"

"Come. Let's get this over with before I change my mind and not let you go at all." She gently pushes me forward.

"What's the doctor's wife like?" I ask as we move slowly up the walk toward the front door.

Nell slows her pace. "I've never given myself the chance of knowing her better. You see, the doctor married her because it was agreed upon between their families. I understand it's the traditional Mexican custom. She's very wealthy from her family's side and she's from Mexico City. So, you two should get along fine.

"You don't like her, do you?"

Her blue eyes snap down at me. "I declare, child, you are certainly a quick picker-upper!"

"What's that, Nell?"

Before she can answer, the door opens and a plump woman in a stiff white apron says, "Yes?" She does not open the door wide, but holds it half-closed, as if guarding the entrance.

Nell answers, "We are here to see Señora Pilar."

The woman's face softens when her eyes meet mine and her cheeks turn pink. "Is she expecting you, Miss Nell?" she asks while studying me.

"Yes, she is, Olga, and don't worry, I shall be civil."

"Come this way." She leads us into a small receiving room, where I sit down on a chair with big arms and a large high back. It is covered with the softest material I have ever felt. I know Anita would love this chair because she would have plenty of room to wiggle around.

The room smells like fresh lemons and in the center sits a curved desk on which there is a photograph of the doctor. Nell approaches the desk and stares at the photograph for a long time, then she moves to the window and plays with a strand of her long hair.

"What is this material called?"

"Velvet, Kata. It's very expensive."

I go to the desk and look at the photograph. "The doctor looks very young in this picture."

Nell stares out the window as if dreaming. "Yes, he was still in medical school back then."

"How do you know?"

She turns quickly. "Oh, Kata, it's a very long story. You don't need to know it, anyway." She peers back out the window. "It would serve no purpose."

I move back to the velvet chair and we settle in silence until the door opens and a woman enters. She glances down at me as she passes and turns her attention to Nell, who seems like a statue frozen in place.

The doctor's wife is tall and very skinny. Taller than Nell, but not as pretty. She is skinny and frail looking, like a willow growing in the middle of a pond. Her hips sway as she walks over to the desk, moves behind it and reaches into the top drawer. She pulls out a cigarette and lights it. I gasp in horror, for Mexican women do not smoke in the presence of others. But it does not disturb this woman dressed in black.

Nell speaks first. "Look Pilar, I've brought the child over as Augustine requested."

Pilar nods, not saying a word as she stares at Nell with dark dagger eyes and then blows a large amount of smoke toward Nell.

Nell clasps her hands and continues, "I trust you will care for her." Then she rushes over to me and bends down to say, "Call me if you need me. I have put my phone number on the card in the bag." She pulls me to her and kisses my cheek. I must go. Be good, Kata. I shall miss you."

Before I can remind her that she did not teach me how to use the black horn, she bolts out the door. I rush to the window and watch her drive out of sight. Then I turn my attention back to the vampire that stands behind me.

"Niña, child, understand that my husband wants you here. I don't care what you do, just so you leave me alone and stay out of my way. If you need anything, speak with Olga, my maid."

I decide that silence is the best answer, so I just nod. I watch her rise like a sleek black cat that is proud of its power. "Olga! Come here!" She stands with her hands on her hips, looking down at me as if she were a poisonous rattler. A very nervous Olga rushes into the room. "Take her to the room we've prepared," Pilar commands.

Olga takes my hand in one of hers and picks up the bag with the other. She rushes out of the room and up the stairs, as if there is a monster after us. She drags me along until we are well out of sight and sound of Pilar.

"Thanks to all the saints!" Olga mutters breathlessly.

"Yes," I rapidly agree.

She chuckles as she pushes open one of the doors that stand in a row along a big hallway. "I think I am going to like you, child." She leads me into a large bedroom. "I will call you in time for supper, because I would not want you to be late. Not even the doctor dares be late. Bless his poor soul." She puts the bag on the bed.

"I don't like her much!" I snap.

Olga laughs. "Not many people do, my child. Stay out of her way and out of the hallway," she warns. "And never wander to that part of the house. Her rooms are to the south end, but you can come to the kitchen any time. Ah, but look, don't you like your room?"

I glance around. "Yes, but why is the bed covered like a big umbrella? Does it rain inside the room?"

Olga roars and her stomach flops up and down. "Oh, dear me! It's not an umbrella, it's called a canopy, like a hood for the bed. It's a bed for the rich people and, I might add, very much trouble to keep clean."

"But, why is a hood needed if there is no sun?"

"It is like a very expensive toy for adults. No sun or rain, just a lot of ruffles and pleats to wash and iron."

"This room is bigger than our hut back home. If we had this room back there, all of the family could live together—even Grandma and Grandpa."

Olga turns, "I believe they could, but rich people

do not like to be close to one another. The doctor has his room and his library for his books and she has her rooms and her dressing room, not to mention all the closets."

"Are you rich, Olga?"

"Heavens no! I only work for the doctor," she chuckles. "But, I have my own room in this house. Now, I must go set the table for dinner. When I have finished I will return for you."

Olga rushes out of the room closing the door behind her. I know she is afraid of Pilar because she seems to walk on the tip of her toes whenever Pilar is near. I will not be afraid, I decide. I'll be like Anita who is brave and bold. I flop down on the big bed and stare up at the white umbrella, wondering what Nell and Ramona were doing and if Betty still cries.

I soon tire of the umbrella bed and of colord tea cups with ugly people painted on them. I long for the books and toys at the center. I lay on the bed and pull out the pouch. The stone seems darker now. I sigh and return it to the pouch.

My stomach begins to rumble, so I sit up and go to the door. I open it just enough to stick out my head and peek down the hall. Olga turns the corner near the stairs. She sees me, waves her arms and says, "Now I will have to dress you for dinner. Have you something clean to wear?"

I open the bag and pull out the dress Nell gave me. The card with her phone number falls out and I pick it up and then stuff it back into the bag. "I have this dress."

"That will do fine. Let me help you change," she offers.

I pull away from her. "I can do it myself!" I order trying to imitate Pilar.

"So, you can. Hurry then, because they will be waiting." She stands there watching me. "Well, get on with it."

"Please leave the room," I ask.

"Oh, no. I dare not. If she sees me in the hall, I'll really get chewed out."

"Okay, then. But, you must turn your back until I'm ready," I demand.

"I'll do anything, just get dressed quickly."

I pull on the dress, then go to her for help in tying the sash at the back of the dress. She does it quickly. We rush out of the room and downstairs to the dining room. "For the saint's sake child, don't speak unless you're asked questions." She's so jittery that she is making me nervous, as well.

The doctor stands at the entrance way. "Hello, Kata. You look lovely. Are you being tended to?"

I glance at Olga, who looks as though she is about to faint. "Yes, I am," I answer. I swear that I heard a sigh escape from plump Olga's lips.

"We have another dinner guest. So, please try to mind your manners. For my wife's sake, you see." He says this in a soft voice and takes my hand to lead me into the dining room, which smells of lemon oil and chicken.

Pilar is already seated next to the guest. She has a smile from ear to ear and is laughing like a silly school girl. She stops when we enter the room.

The doctor introduces me. "Don Francisco, this is my temporary charge, Katarina Campos."

The man with the thick black hair and very straight nose rises and bows. "What a lovely child," he says more to the doctor than to me. Then he reseats himself, glad to forget me, it seems. He immediately turns his attention back to the cat-woman, Pilar.

The doctor leads me to a chair and sits next to me. Pilar starts laughing again like a crazy witch, stirring her boiling potion. The doctor should tell her to behave, I think, but I notice he seems to ignore his wife and concentrate on his glass of wine. Don Francisco, I notice, is all eyes and ears, like the big bad wolf ready to eat up Pilar.

Dinner is served very quickly by Olga. Pilar and Don Francisco keep their whispering jokes to their side of the table and the doctor concentrates on his food, occasionally smiling down at me.

Doctor Mendez looks tired. I can tell by the rings under his eyes and the way he slouches on his chair. He is too young to have those rings, I think, as I watch him take a second glass of wine. This is not how my Mama and Papa act during meals. I've seen them kiss countless times before and during meals.

By the time Olga brings the ice cream, I have decided that the doctor does not care what his wife does nor does she care about him. The doctor must have read my mind, for when our eyes meet he looks quickly away.

After I finish my ice cream, the doctor asks, "Kata, would you like to go for a walk with me?"

"Yes!" I say quickly, for I do not want him to change his mind. I am tired of being inside and I long for the open air. I scoop up the remaining ice cream and stand. He takes my hand and leads me out of the dining room. He doesn't bother to tell Pilar or Don Francisco that we are leaving, but I don't think they will have noticed anyway.

As we walk in the evening twilight I notice the

doctor's silence and say, "Cola del gato! Tail of a cat!" He was very much surprised, for no words had passed between us. "Does the cat have his tail in your mouth?" I ask. "You do not speak."

"I see." He smiles and removes his pipe. "Well, Kata. I have my problems and worries to think about, as you can probably tell."

"But with all this wealth you should not have problems."

"That is not so, child. Even the rich have common problems."

"Still, I can see that you are not happy."

"Happy, a child's word. Still, I believe I was the happiest when I was a poor medical student." He stopped walking and leaned against a fence post.

"You don't like Pilar, nor does Olga, nor Nell. That must be part of the problem, or else you would smile more."

He laughs, "That's three strikes against Pilar. But, Nell would dislike her the most."

"Yes, I believe they could have killed each other this afternoon. Nell left very quickly after Pilar blew smoke into her face. Have they always disliked each other?"

"It's all my fault. You see, I wanted to marry Nell long ago, but that was before Pilar came to live with me."

"That's the reason they don't like each other?"

"What I should have done is sent Pilar back home and married Nell, but I chickened out, simply because I felt I owed Pilar's family for financing some of my education." He took a long puff and blew little circles of smoke into the air. "Also, Nell being Anglo, I felt that it might hurt my practice. Stupid, it was all so stupid."

"Did you ever kiss Nell?"

"Yes, many times and I found it very enjoyable."

"My Mama and Papa kiss all the time. They say it's fun, but I've never kissed a boy, just Pablito, my baby brother."

"Some day you'll kiss a boy, but you must remember to marry from the heart, not the mind. The mind, you see, as brilliant as it is, plays tricks, but the heart remains true."

"I would have noticed that Nell and Anita do not like each other also."

"You have to understand that Nell is Anglo and she doesn't understand lots of Mexican folk customs, but she tries to learn. Look how she's mastered the Spanish language."

"Yes, she speaks good Spanish. I believe I like Nell much better than Pilar and I like Anita much better than Nell, but Mama and Papa I like best of all."

The doctor laughs, "You children! You make life so simple, as if it were a ladder to climb up and down."

I glanced up at him and studied his face for a second before I asked, "Why don't you send Pilar home? Then you can take Nell and marry her."

"I doubt Nell would have me now. And besides, grown-up ways are not so simple, Kata. Would you trade your mother for another one if you didn't like her?"

"No, because she loves me," I declare. "And Nell still likes you. I can see it in her eyes each time you pass her."

"Well, perhaps so, but I think deep inside Pilar loves me."

I shake my head as I climb onto the fence to sit. "I don't think so, doctor. She likes Don Francisco more.

Ask her yourself," I suggest.

He coughs and taps his heart. "I just might do that." He lifts me off the fence and takes my hand. On the front porch he says, "Goodnight, Kata. Sleep tight." He turns to the door and shouts, "Olga, please take Kata to her room."

From the top of the stairs I look back to see that he is still outside, looking up at the stars and rubbing the back of his neck. Once in my room, I hear a car engine start up. I dash over to the window to catch a glimpse of him putting the car into reverse. Poor doctor, I think, as I watch the tail lights of his car zip down the drive, like a wet snake disappering under a rock. Pilar probably doesn't know that he has left, since her eyes are all wrapped up in Don Francisco.

Chapter Nine

I lie upon the umbrella bed thinking of Anita and Pablito. I can see him sucking his thumb as he lies asleep on the bed of straw. Anita will be lying on her back, snoring and gasping at the same time. The summer moonlight floods the room through open windows and a breeze freshens the air. I spread my arms out as far as they can go and still cannot reach the ends of the big bed. I wonder if Anita would snore in this bed or even if she could sleep confortably. I move over to one side of the bed. Yes, I think, there is plenty of room for both Anita and Pablito.

I push the pillows off the bed and lay flat on my back, watching the ruffles above me sway gently as the breeze seems to kiss them goodnight. I wish Papa were here to kiss me goodnight. As I fall into sleep I hear Papa call to me as he used to do back in Mexico.

Anita once said that dreams can be made real if one wishes it. I will wish for Papa to come visit me in my dreams tonight and for him to lift me into the air like he used to. I close my eyes tightly and clutch the pouch, forcing myself to think only of Papa. But the dream does not come nor does sleep. I snap my eyes open and slowly sit up. I turn over on my stomach and stare into the moonlight. Soon, I fall asleep.

In my dream Papa comes, but he is wet and hungry. His eyes are huge and seem to stare into the distance. He cries for help as he runs to me with his arms outstretched, but he passes me as if I were not standing there at all. "Papa!" I scream, but he continues to run. I watch as he runs out of sight, growing smaller and smaller in the ghostly distance. My head hangs to my chest and my arms fall to my side. Papa has disappeared from sight and, in sadness, I turn to walk away.

When I look up again, I see a small black object growing larger as it shortens the distance between us. I can see it is some sort of animal, a cat, a black cat. Dust rises as each of its paws pounce on the ground. It rapidly approaches me, but I cannot move out of its path. Perhaps it's chasing Papa, I think, but its huge front paws knock me down on my back and pin me under them. The cat licks my face clean with its sponge-like tongue, as if tasting me, and then it crawls on top of my chest staring at my eyes and mouth, as if deciding which one to eat first.

With each moment that passes the cat becomes heavier and heavier. Soon I am gasping for breath and I begin to struggle with it. I try to push it off with my arms, but it remains unmoveable, yet constantly staring at my mouth.

"Anita!" I scream, as I cover my face with my arms. Immediately after I call out to Anita, the cat springs off of me. It scampers into the darkness and I awake covered with sweat and frozen in fear. Anita said to pray whenever I am frightened, so I pray over and over again until daylight floods the room.

I awake when Olga enters the room. "Good morning," she sings. "Did you sleep well?"

I follow her movements with my eyes, not bothering to answer. I feel weak, so I close my eyes for a moment of relief.

Olga closes the windows. "Not ready to rise? Well that's fine. Sleep late, child. We have plenty of time before we visit the hospital." She straightens the blanket, takes my hand. "My, you look pale." She touches my forehead. "But, you're not running a fever, which is good."

"Olga," I whisper. "Stay with me until I sleep."

She chuckles, "If that's what you want, but only for a moment. I have many other things to do." She clamps her hand on my wrist and smiles down at me.

When I awake I find that Olga has gone. Feeling better, I dress myself and go downstairs. Olga is in the kitchen humming a tune. "What would you like to eat?" she asks. "I've made some fresh hot oatmeal."

I nod and sit where she directs. She continues to whistle as she serves me. "Eat quickly because we have to visit your Mama." She brings me a cup of sweet coffee and some orange juice. "I called Doctor Mendez and told him you seemed a bit tired. He said to let you get all the sleep you needed, then to drive you to the hospital. I am to wait with you until your visit is over."

I take a spoonful of oatmeal, then glance up. "And, where is she . . . Señora Pilar?"

"Ah, bad news. And I guess it could be good news, too. It seems the good doctor did not come home last night and the señora is very upset."

"She doesn't seem to care for him anyway," I add, taking a spoonful of oatmeal and putting it in my mouth.

"Maybe, but she fears a scandal will hurt her precious family name . . . but that is none of our affair. Come on, child. Eat!"

I slam my spoon down. "Olga!" I cry, "you hurry me so much that you're beginning to tire me out!"

On hearing my outburst, her hand comes down upon her heart as if she'd been stabbed. "I am sorry, child," she says softly. "I must learn to slow down for my own sake. Sometimes I believe that I've worked here much too long. I don't mean to act nervous, but Señora Pilar is always on my nerves," she continues, as if talking to herself. "Before he married her, this house was gay with laughter and laziness. Miss Nell, she made him laugh a lot. Now he never laughs."

"Olga, he's sad, that's all."

"True, oh, but he needs to take his mind off his work. If he continues as he is, he will grow old before his time. You mark my words!" She wipes her hands on her apron. "Now that you're finished, I'll put my apron on the rack and we'll be off. It's nice to be going somewhere, since I seldom get a chance to leave this house."

"Yes, I'm ready to see Mama again," I say, hoping that she is better.

Olga and I find Mama unmoving, yet staring at the ceiling. I, too, look up searching for whatever she sees, but I find nothing of interest. Olga straightens Mama's sheets while I talk about things that have happened since she fell ill. After ten minutes, Olga motions for us to leave and I kiss Mama goodbye.

"I don't think she'll ever be well again, Olga." I cry once we are out of the room.

"Yes, she will, child. She needs time and lots of care."

"Anita said that too."

"Then she is a wise woman."

I take Olga's hand, "And so are you, Olga."

That afternoon I play outside in the doctor's large

flower garden. My favorite spot is far removed from the rest of the garden. There stands a small house with benches that one can sit upon and gaze at various rocks and flowers. Olga finds me there.

"Kata, come, it is almost time for supper."

I take her hand as we walk back toward the house. Olga does not seem to be in a hurry, instead she strolls glancing at flowers on each side of the walk. "Olga," I ask, "will the doctor be here for supper?"

She sighs, "Señora Pilar is eating out tonight and the doctor has other plans. You and I shall have supper together."

I am disappointed, for I liked speaking with him. "I wish he would come home, Olga."

"I spoke with him on the phone earlier, and he sounded very happy, lots gayer than I've seen him in a long time." She puts her arm over my shoulder. "But, we shall have a very good supper tonight and it will be held in my favorite place . . . my own kitchen! Besides, with you here, I shall not be eating alone."

"You are right!" I clasp my hands. "I love your kitchen, Olga, and I hate that dining room. Have you a piece of cake in your kitchen?" I ask, winking up at her.

"If there's not a piece already baked, we can spend tonight making a fresh one."

"A whole cake! Can you show me how to make one, so that I can teach Mama when she gets well."

"I most certainly will." She takes my hand and we walk slowly up the path toward her kitchen.

That evening, Olga and I decide to make a chocolate cake. I pull up a stool and watch as Olga explains all the things that go into a cake. They are called "ingredients."

We continue working and are only disturbed by the sound of a car starting up. "The señora must be leaving," says Olga without stopping her work.

It is late when Olga and I sit together on stools to eat a slice or two of her cake. It is good, but not as delicious as Ramona's.

The black cat comes again that night. This time I fall harder into the dirt, and it is even heavier upon my chest. I kick with my legs and shove with my arms, but the cat stands strong, refusing to leave my chest. My eyes feel like bursting and I gasp for air with my mouth open wide. The cat seems to enjoy peeking down my throat and watching me struggle.

When I scream Anita's name, the cat jumps off my chest and disappears into the darkness. I lie still, trying to get air back into my empty lungs. Then I tremble and cry out loudly, "Anita!" I scream over and over again.

"Katarina! What's wrong?" questions Olga as she turns on the lights and pulls off the blankets. "You're wet and shaking." She covers me, then rushes out of the room. I hear her pounding on the door down the hall. "Doctor! Come quick! The girl is ill!" she yells.

I try to sit up, but I cannot. The doctor rushes into the room. "Olga!" he orders. "Get these wet things off her. Do it quickly while I go downstairs to get my bag."

Olga's fingers work quicky as she changes me into a clean gown. She carries me over to a big chair and sits me there while she makes the bed. "Don't worry child. The doctor will take good care of you," she says softly. She lifts me back into bed and makes sure that the blanket is snug around me. "Dear me, I wonder what's taking him so long?"

"Olga, please close the door and the windows. Don't let that cat in here again. Please!" I beg.

"Calm yourself, Kata. We don't have cats here. The señora hates cats." She turns as the doctor enters the room.

"Move aside, man! I am needed here!" yells Anita.

"You've come!" I cry out.

She clutches her medicine bag to her chest and hurries to the bed. "I felt you needed me, Kata. Since last night I have had to fight the urge to come out here, but tonight I really knew that you needed me badly." She puts her cloth bag down on the corner of the bed.

Olga lifts her hand to her face and says, "Doctor, who is this?"

The doctor ignores her question and walks to the bed. He puts his bag on the night table. "You can go, Olga. We'll look after Kata."

Olga closes the door as quietly as she can. Anita pulls down the blankets and studies my chest and each of my legs.

"Anita, where is Pablito?" I ask in a whisper.

Anita smiles and pats my hand. "I sent for Don Juan to come stay while I make this trip in his truck." Her smile fades. "I saw the cat in your dreams. A black cat with a black soul is no challenge for a small girl like yourself."

The doctor pulls up a chair closer to the bed and sits watching Anita work. He reaches over and takes my wrist while he stares down at his pocket watch.

"Anita, I could not breathe."

"I must see your back." She turns me gently and grunts, then straightens the blanket. She pokes around in her bag and finally pulls up a red scarf and carefully unties it. "This should do just fine. I guarantee you will sleep tonight." In her hand she holds a large yellow lemon, the largest and brightest I have ever seen. She sits the lemon on the table and searches her bag for a small tan bottle. She opens it and sniffs. "A drop of this on your tongue before we apply the lemon."

It tastes bitter, and I pull away from her hold. I turn to the doctor, who sits back in the chair watching with curious eyes. Anita jerks the blanket from me with a quick snap of her wrist and then she pulls off the gown. She rolls the lemon over every inch of my body. I scream out, for it feels as if she is rubbing a block of frozen ice over me.

"Anita," questions the doctor, "is this necessary?"

"For the cure to work, it must be done. It hurts me too, doctor."

"But I don't understand what this technique does."

"Someone has cast the evil eye upon her, and this ritual draws the evil from her body. This method is as old as the world and it works, it works."

The doctor rises and feels my forehead. "Perhaps you are just adding to her hysteria and upsetting her more."

"Perhaps!" snaps Anita. "But you shall have your time with her after I finish." She stares at him until he turns his back and sits down again.

Anita finishes rubbing me and makes wide circles with the lemon. It seems she is drawing a giant halo over my entire body, then she takes the lemon and carefully puts it in a glass ashtray that sits on the table near the bed. From her bag she pulls out a box of matches. She strikes one sets the flame under the lemon. The flame seems to want to die out, but Anita holds it firm to the lemon. Soon it seems the lemon begins to breathe, growing larger, then rapidly smaller. My eyes blur as Anita begins to chant under her breath, "Away with you, away to your world," she says, over and over again.

The lemon expands like a ballon being filled and presently it begins to hiss as if it has a slow leak. The flame becomes larger and burns the lemon until there is nothing left but a faint smell.

"Remarkable!" exclaims the doctor as he rises to witness the disappearance.

"Ah," says Anita, "perhaps you will believe a little more in my medicine." She turns, "Look, her color returns. Now she shall sleep well for many nights."

The doctor takes my wrist and studies his pocket watch. "Yes, I can see the difference in the pulse rate, but I still believe it is because she believes in you as a curer."

"Anita," I interrupt, "stay tonight."

Anita takes my wrist and upon it she ties a bracelet made of seeds. "What is this?" I ask.

"Something I made for you. It's a charm to ward off all evil. It has six seeds, three small red and white seeds and three very large red and white seeds. Wear it always, Kata. Now rest, for I must return the truck to Don Juan. Pablito waits on me, too. I am with you always." She gathers her cloth bag and her bottles and bends to kiss me. "You will feel well in the morning, and so shall your mother. I have seen her, too, and have given her my tea."

The doctor leaves with Anita, but I can hear her as she carefully makes her way down the stairs. "Doctor Mendez, perhaps you should attend Mass more often," she commands.

He laughs, "And perhaps I should study medicine with you, Doña Anita."

"It might do you some good, my friend, not to mention the good it will do your patients," she adds.

"Nevertheless, I shall be watching Kata all night long."

"So be it," she says.

The following morning I awake feeling that I could run for miles and never tire and could jump the largest of rocks and never step on one. I can remember Anita tending me, but not much else.

"Olga," I say after entering the kitchen, "I am starved. I will eat anything."

She smiles, then feels my forehead. "Good, Kata, because you are the only one I have to cook for."

"Where's Pilar?" I ask, taking a piece of toast.

"She has not returned since yesterday. The doctor left me a note to pack her things up. I understand she called to have all her things sent back to her home in Mexico."

"Really! I am glad! Now he can be with Miss Nell like he wants to be!"

"Is that what he wants?" asks Olga in a very interested voice.

"Yes, and where is the doctor anyway?"

"He's been at the hospital since early this morning. They called him in for emergency surgery. That, added to your little problem last night, should make him fit for a couple of day's sleep. She reaches for her saucepan. "Katarina!" she snaps, "stop eating all that butter or you shall become as fat as that old witch that visited you last night."

"She is not an old witch, Olga. She is my friend and I love her like a grandmother . . . even if she is fat and ugly."

Olga stares at me for a moment, then her face brightens as a smile breaks. "I don't care what she is, as long as she did you some good." She hands me a plate. You see, the doctor and I had late coffee together and he explained everything after she left. It seems he thinks a lot of her in a mysterious sort of way."

"Mysterious? What is that?"

"It means that he likes her and respects her, but can't really figure her out. You know, like you really can't figure out all the facts about God."

"I see. Anita is very close to God, and she knows the devil, too. But she loves God enough to do his fighting against the devil."

"Oh, I would not like to be in her shoes!" Olga adds, then quickly crosses herself.

I beg Olga to take me to see Mama that afternoon. She finally calls the doctor and he gives his okay. I find that Mama seems to hear me better. She slowly turns her head to me as if she can hear me, but can't see me.

"Mama! Hear me. Wake up, it's me, Kata!" I repeat it again.

"Give her time, Kata," advises Olga as she changes the water on the stand.

"Time. She should be awake by now. Anita said so," I snap.

"No one is perfect, Kata. Every person is different. If I'd been in your Mama's shoes, I'd probably be sleeping until next Christmas."

"Next Christmas! I can't wait that long!" I howl.

"It's just a joke, Kata," adds Olga.

"Mama!" I repeat. "Wake up, Mama."

As I study her face, a small smile appears and her eyes seem to move from one side to the other. She turns her head several times and then she blinks. "Kata," she says after her eyes have cleared.

"Mama! You're awake at last! Oh, Mama, how I've missed you." I hug her tightly.

Olga immediately leaves the room and within seconds Doctor Mendez rushes inside. "Señora," he says, "do not move until I have checked you entirely." I watch as he examines her head, her eyes and the rest of her body. As he does, he talks in a soothing tone, "Kata is here as you can see, but Pablito is with Anita out at her rancho."

"I dreamed that Anita came to me last night," whispers Mama. "May I have a drink of water?"

He holds her glass and puts the straw in her mouth, then moves away from the bed. "Well, Kata, she is better. I believe the ice has finally been broken. Now, I can really work on getting her on her feet."

"Her hands are very cold," I say.

"That is expected, but remember her recovery is going to take time. I told you that once, but her waking is a very good sign."

"Mama," I add, "Anita was here last night. I saw her myself."

A puzzled look crosses her eyes. "I dreamed she gave me a tea . . . a very sweet tea."

"She told me she did. Didn't she, doctor?"

"Yes, Kata, she did, and I believe her medicine is just as good as mine . . . sometimes, given the proper circumstances."

The door creaks open and Nell peeks around the corner. "May I come in?"

"Sure." The doctor rushes over to lead her in by the elbow. "We have great news. Kata's mother is conscious."

"That is good, Kata," she says as she approaches the bed.

"Nell!" I hug her around the waist. "How I've missed you and Ramona."

Nell pats my back and gives me another hug. "We've missed you too, Kata."

I hear Mama sigh heavily, so I rush to her. "This time, Mama, please take better care of yourself."

"Yes, Kata. You are right."

I notice her voice seems small and distant. "Don't worry about a thing, Mama. I'm right here and I will take care of you, and when Papa comes back, he'll take care of all of us."

Tears wet her eyes. "Have you found Carlos?"

"No, Mama, but we will. We have to," I answer, smoothing back her hair.

She clutches my hand and clears her throat again. "You sound sure of yourself, my little Kata. How you've grown since we left the village. You're not a little girl anymore."

"I hate to interrupt," adds the doctor, "but, she must rest. Kata, say goodbye. The nurse must tend to her needs."

"I'll be back tomorrow, Mama." I hug her, then follow Nell and Olga out of the room. Out in the hall I stop. "Hasn't it been a perfect day?"

Olga chuckles, "As perfect as can be!"

Nell mutters, "The best ever!"

I glance up to see that she beams like a rainbow in the heavens. "You do love him!" I shout happily.

Nell stops walking, "Kata, you are a remarkable girl."

And Olga answers, "Very remarkable," and they both laugh.

Chapter Ten

Doctor Mendez finally announces that Mama is well enough to go home. He arranges for a man to drive us out to the ranchito. "See to it that your mother rests, Kata," he orders.

Mama has been in low spirits all week long. I think it is because she feels she has failed in this new land. I try to cheer her up, but it does no good. Instead, it is Nell who is able to snap her out of it.

"Señora!" declares Nell late one afternoon, "see what I have brought you." She lays a large box on Mama's lap. "Untie it," she urges.

Mama gasps in surprise. "New dresses for Kata and ... and for me. You shouldn't have done this. They must have cost you a lot of money."

"Doctor Mendez asked me to buy them for you and for Kata. He was the one that paid for them, but I chose them. You see, he seldom gets to go shopping. If you do not like one, tell me, and I shall return it for another."

"No, no, they are all beautiful. Thank you, Miss Nell."

"Thanks to Doctor Mendez. He has also paid the hospital bill for you and is not going to charge you a cent for his services. Isn't that sweet of him?"

"Yes, but why does he do all this for us? We have done nothing for the man but cause him problems."

"I believe we might safely say that Kata saved his life, right Kata?" she winks at me.

"No, I just told him Pilar doesn't like him," I add, confused.

Nell laughs and hugs me tightly. "What a girl you are, Kata."

Mama sits up in the bed. "When do we leave, Miss Nell?"

Nell sighs. "I'm afraid it's tomorrow morning."

I clap my hands. "Good. I will get to see Anita and Pablito soon, but I will miss you, Nell and Ramona."

"Well, we might go visit you now that Ramona knows where Anita lives."

"She does . . . how?"

"Anita gave her directions out to the ranch. She went out there yesterday to speak with Anita about babies."

"Then, you shall be visiting us soon."

"I think very soon, Kata," smiles Nell.

I am glad to be going back to the ranchito. I will miss Olga and the doctor as I miss the gift of quietness that Anita's place offers. But for me, our little village in Mexico will always be my home, no matter where I go or whom I meet."

The next morning I shake the doctor's hand and give Nell a big hug and kiss. I hurry to the waiting car and wave to them as the car pulls out. I feel happy for them, but sad to be leaving them, also.

As the ride lengthens, I find myself staring out of the car window. Silently I watch the hot desert pass before me. I sigh, "Mama, I would like to go home and see grandmother and grandfather."

"So would I, Kata. It's been hard on us here. What would we have done without dear Anita? We owe her a lot." She places her arms around my shoulders and kisses the top of my head.

"Maybe Anita can help us get back home. Do you think she can?"

"Perhaps, Kata. But I have no money." She sobs. "I want to go back home and see my folks just as much as you do."

"We'll find a way once you are better. I am sure
Anita will help us."

Mama stops crying and laughs a little. "Ah,
Kata. What a child you are. A true dreamer, just like
your Papa."

I complain, "Yesterday you called me all grown
up. Today I am a child again. I think you older people
are the ones that are all mixed up! You change as
quickly as the sun and the moon change places at
night."

Mama laughs, "I believe you are right, Kata."

As we drive into the ranchito, Anita waves franti-
cally, for she has seen us coming. She throws off her
apron and picks up Pablito in her arms. Mama is
right, I think, as I watch Anita tumble toward us. We
belong to her, too.

"Thanks be to the heavenly saints!" she cries.
"You are both home safely." She opens the car door to
help Mama out. "Kata, my baby! Pablito and I have
missed you."

I take Pablito into my arms. He pokes his fingers
in my mouth and pulls my hair. "Ouch! You have not
changed one bit, Pablito!" I scold as I take him over to
the porch.

Anita offers the driver a drink, but he declines,
saying that he needs to get back to town as soon as
possible. All four of us stand on the porch watching
him disappear down the dusty road. Mama's face
seems pinched, as though she is seeing part of her life
fade into the past, and upon Anita's face I see a smile
as big as a pumpkin while she pats her fat stomach in
a very satisfied manner. I sit myself down on the
porch steps and sigh, because I find peace in this barren countryside, except for Pablito who stands behind

me choking my throat and pulling my pigtails.

Anita must think that we are starved to death, because that evening she fixes a huge supper of enchiladas covered with cheese and onions, beans, rice and tacos. She also has a surprise for us . . . cold tea.

"Anita," I ask "how did you get the tea this cold?"

She giggles, "I outsmarted myself, no?"

"Yes, you did, Anita. Now tell us how," asks Mama.

"I sealed the tea in a big jar, put it inside the bucket that belongs to the well and lowered it into the cold well water. I let it stay there all day. See, I felt you would be coming home today."

"That's a great idea, Anita. I shall always remember that."

"Have you heard anything about Carlos?" asks Mama.

Anita puts down her plate of food, then sits herself in the chair opposite Mama. "I have asked around. But as yet I have not heard a thing. I left word at several places for those two scoundrels to get back with me."

"Yes, perhaps they know something of him," responds Mama.

"Anita," I interrupt, "do you think you could help us get back home?" I watch as she stiffens. "I mean find a way to get us back to Mexico."

She sighs, then speaks slowly as if she is thinking hard. "I think we could get you back across, if that's what you want." She glances at Mama with lowered eyes, not wanting her to say what she knew she had to say.

Mama answers just as cautiously, "It's just that we are so unfamiliar with the American ways and customs. In Mexico, our village life was so simple and happier." She puts her hand on Anita's shoulder. "I hope I have not hurt you by wanting to return."

"No, I understand why. I live out here for the peace of mind it brings me, for I am a free person, and thus it should be with your little village home."

I interrupt again. "I really want to go home. I've even lost my Anna and I don't now where," I wail.

Anita throws back her head and howls in laughter. Her breasts shake and her bad eye blinks, "Poor Anna! I found her in the room all alone. So I stuffed her in a sack and brought her back here." She rises quickly and goes over to the closet. "See, here is poor Anna."

I scream as I reach her and I crush her to my chest, then hold her at a distance to examine her dress, which is wrinkled but not torn. "Anna, you're home, too."

Mama rises and puts her arms around Anita. "I think we are all ready to go back home. Do you think you can help us?"

I look up from smoothing Anna's dress. "If we need money, we can sell the pretty stone."

"What stone?" asks Mama turning sharply toward me.

"The one that was in the pouch." I lift my skirt and undo the pouch.

Mama's eyes bulge out. "I thought I had lost that pouch!"

"No, I had it all the time, Mama." I hold the pouch upside down and the stone falls into my palm. "It's a little pretty isn't it, Anita? Maybe we can get three or four American dollars for it."

123

Anita takes the stone from me and holds it to the light. "Maybe so, little one." She softly whistles and turns to Mama. "Do you know what kind of stone this is?"

"I never have seen it, but I remember Carlos putting something in the pouch before we left the village."

"It was in the pouch when we got to the river. That man that Papa handed the money to saw it also. I know he wanted it because he asked Papa about it." I put the pouch down on the table. "Anyway, I'm glad that I do not have to wear that old thing any longer. It scratches me."

Anita chuckles, "I have a close friend that knows about rocks and stones. I will take it to him tomorrow. Perhaps, he can help."

Mama shrugs, "So be it, señora."

"It may bring a good price. Enough, perhaps, to get you back to your village." Anita turns to the bed and pulls down the blanket. "If you go back, I will come visit."

"Anita, you can come any time you please." I kiss her hand. "After all, you found Anna." I take my doll to our straw bed and play with her until Mama turns out the lantern.

The next morning Anita sets out to her friend's house. "I will be gone all day. I should be back a little after dark. If I do not return, it is because they have asked me to stay for the night. So, do not worry, for I will return the following morning."

I watch her bulky figure sway back and forth as

she walks off into the distance. Soon she is a tiny speck against the tan horizon.

"Kata, feed the chickens. We have to help Anita with her work," says Mama.

"All right, Mama. I'll take Pablito so that he can learn how to do it."

When I glance back up the road, Anita has disappeared.

Two days pass and Anita has not returned. Mama is sick with worry and so am I. We have no idea where she has gone and with each minute that passes Mama bites harder on her fingernails and I walk one more time out to the porch to look down the road.

After lunch on the third day, Anita bursts through the screen door. "Heavens!" she pants. "What luck!" She breathes heavily, but undoes her scarf, as if she were opening a surprise package. She flings her shawl upon the back of the chair as if it were a dishtowel.

"Anita! Where have you been?" scolds Mama.

"Never mind. I go several places, not just one. My friend told me he thought the stone to be a gold nugget, but maybe it could be fool's gold, too. He was not all that sure, so he sent me to another of his friends who is a jeweler in town. He said it was real and offered to buy it right off."

"You're telling jokes, Anita. Where would Carlos get a gold nugget?" questions Mama standing with her hands on her hips.

"I don't know. But I do know that it is real. The man bought it without questions." She flops her cloth bag on the table. "Look!" She jerks open the bag and rolls of green money flow forth.

"Anita!" shouts Mama, "where on earth did you get so much money?"

"I just told you. Weren't you listening?" she cries. "It's all yours. The man bought the gold nugget for $600 American dollars."

"Bless all the saints! Kata, now we can go back home!" screams Mama for joy as she lifts me into the air.

"Yes," beams Anita like an old lantern. "And with enough money to buy a piece of land, some cows and some chickens. Perhaps even open a store in your village."

"If only Carlos were here! He'd know what to do with all that money," cries Mama sadly.

I look up at her and shrug, then I take a fistful of bills and smell them. They smell stale like old bread, but they will get us home. "I know what to do with it, Mama. Don't worry."

"Yes, you would, Kata," she sniffles. "You've grown so much lately."

I glance up quickly and smirk. "That is very funny, because yesterday you called me a child and today I'm all grown up again. You big people never make up your mind," I snap, picking up Anna from the table and kissing her. "Except you, Anita. You always know what to do."

In two days, Anita has arranged for our trip home. "This time, you shall leave this country by the right method. We will take a bus over the border. I

126

will go along with my papers just in case. But I believe we shall have no problem at all."

"Hurray!" I shout, "a bus ride into Mexico! Fantastico!" I dance around, taking Pablito into a swirl.

Anita chuckles. "Once we have crossed, I shall find my friend who is a big man with many connections. He has agreed to meet us and drive us personally to your village."

"Anita, you are an angel sent from heaven!" declares Mama.

"Oh, no . . . not an angel. Just an old healer sent to this world to help. Besides, this man owes me several favors for helping his family in their time of need. He is just paying his dues, even if he is a commandante with the Mexican army."

"Do you mean someone that important will drive us back home? Won't Juanita and Estela be surprised to see me come home in a big fancy car?" I squeal. "When do we leave?"

Anita quickly turns to stir the pot on the stove. "Friday morning."

Mama gasps, "Why that's tomorrow morning!"

"So it is," answers Anita.

Mama's face is lit up like a candle that glows in the dark, but Anita's face hangs in sadness. I walk over and put my forehead against her hip and say nothing.

Later that night I watch Anita sew Anna a new dress. Between two layers of cloth she sews many of the bills. "This is just in case something should happen. It is best to be always prepared." My face falls and she quickly adds, "Oh, you still can play with Anna when I am finished, but don't tell a soul what's inside her dress."

"I promise, Anita. I just want to hold her on the

bus."

"There, her dress is all ready. The rest of the money, I shall carry." She stares down at Anna for a moment, then sighs heavily.

"Aren't you happy, Anita?" I ask, noticing her quietness.

"For you, yes. But for me, no. I have become like a grandma to you and Pablito. I have come to think of you all as my adopted family and I will miss everyone." She wipes her brow with her apron sash. "But, I will not rest until I have delivered you safely to your village."

"Why don't you move to Mexico with us. You would like it in our little village."

"This is my home, Kata, and I cannot leave it for very long. I have explained all that before. I have my ranchito and my patients and you have your life before you."

"Yes, that is true, Anita. But I am still worried about Papa. Have you heard anything?"

She shakes her head. "I have not heard a thing." She slowly sticks her needle and thread into the cushion.

We are up early the next day, fixing tacos filled with beans for our trip. After we have packed our belongings into bags, Don Juan arrives and we pile into the truck ready for the trip into town.

"Are you ready, old woman?" Don Juan snaps at Anita.

"Of course, I am, you goat! Get in yourself so that we may be on the road before the sun fully rises."

Don Juan chuckles to himself. "I like your spirit, old woman!"

Anita growls, "Don Juan, please just shut up! And drive this truck or I shall do it myself!"

Mama holds up both her arms. "Let's not argue on our last day together."

Don Juan turns red, "Well, you see how that old woman sticks me with that tongue of hers. Hump! We shall see who shall miss who!"

Anita roars, "I shall never miss you, señor."

I interrupt to say, "Mama, don't you think they should get married to each other. So they won't be alone."

Mama claps her hands. "What a wonderful idea. They would make a handsome couple, and it's never too late for marriage."

"Marriage!" cries Anita. "Why the old rooster has no fight left in him!"

"Now, Anita," mutters Mama, "I see signs that speak otherwise."

"What signs!" she argues.

"My, my. How you blush at your age!" giggles Mama.

Anita flaps her arms wildly. "Enough of this silly talk. Enough, I say!"

We arrive in town and Don Juan slowly makes his way to the bus station. There he waits, like the gentleman he is, for us to board the bus. "Old woman," he says, "be careful!"

"I shall, old man," answers Anita as she touches his hand gently. "If I should not return, the ranchito is yours."

"Why would I want that God-forsaken piece of land?" Don Juan slaps his straw hat against his leg.

"Because I give it to you!" commands Anita in a

huff as she boards the bus.

The excitement of the bus ride soon dies out, as our ride approaches the fourth hour. The land out the window becomes more barren and I can see hazy heat rise from the sand.

"Anita," I ask, "how much longer?"

"Another couple of hours. It's a bit longer by bus than cutting straight across the river like you did. Now rest, child."

On the seat behind us, Mama and Pablito are napping. I wiggle until I find a comfortable position and close my eyes.

"Stop!" shouts a deep voice.

I sense the bus has stopped. I rouse myself slowly and find Anita looking out the window. "Hold tightly to Anna and don't let anyone have her," she instructs.

"Stop for inspection! All passengers must get out of the bus while it is inspected and sprayed. All luggage and bags must be inspected, so take them with you," shouts the voice.

As quickly as I can say "enchiladas!" a soldier comes hurrying down the aisle of the bus. He carries a very long rifle which is slung across his back and on his hip swings a gun in a holster. He looks right and left, occasionally nodding or asking a person his name. He stares hard when he comes to Anita, but she stares right back. He goes on until he reaches the back of the bus. Satisfied, he hurries down the aisle, then spends a few seconds talking to the driver before he turns and says, "Everyone must get out now. Take your belongings with you."

"Darn it!" hisses Anita as she gathers the things. She waits until everyone else has left the bus, then she rises and makes her way out. I follow clutching Anna to my chest.

We enter a small brick building where the people are already lined up. One by one their luggage and bags are opened and checked. I watch as they mess up all the clothes, then slam the bag shut without bothering to straighten the clothes. Then they summon the next person and repeat everything again.

"What are they looking for?" I ask.

"There are certain things, like plants, fruits and animals that one is not allowed to take across the border. They also look for guns and drugs which they take from you."

I notice that all the guards carry pistols and rifles. Even the ones checking the bags, and they frown as if they hate doing their job.

As Anita approaches the guard, he smiles at her. "Good day, señora," he says.

Anita stares at him. "Do I know you?"

"No, señora, but I know you and your cures."

"And how is this?" questions Anita.

"You tended my old uncle who was bit by a desert spider."

"Oh, and how is your uncle now?" questions Anita as she pops her bag upon the counter.

"Dead now," he answers, then adds, "but not from your cure. He died from old age." He opens the bag and shuffles through it. "I hope he rests with the good Lord," he adds, then stops and glances up at Anita. Slowly he pulls out a small bottle. "What is this, my good señora?"

"A tonic for curing the swelling of the throat and ankles. I am to see another patient in Mexico."

He opens the bottle and smells it and quickly re-closes it. "You shall pass. Has the child anything to search?"

Anita turns to me. "Nothing but her cloth doll."

I gasp and look from Anita to the guard and then clutch Anna tighter to me.

"It's all right, little girl. You don't have to part with your doll. Just run along with the señora." He glances up at Anita and tips his hat. "Have a nice trip."

"And luck be with you," smiles Anita with a slight bow.

We are the last to board the bus, and I can see that Mama has been biting her nails again. Once we are safely seated and well on the road, Mama says to Anita, "I was so worried."

"Everything worked out fine. The trip should run smoothly until we meet my friend," says Anita. "And, thanks be to the Lord," she adds in a whisper.

It is well into the middle of the afternoon when we finally arrive at the meeting place. The Commandante is waiting and takes Anita's hand to help her into the front seat of the big black car. We pile into the back seat, he starts the car and we speed out of town. It seems unusual that he, an important officer, does not have a driver. He talks rapidly in a very nervous manner and his right hand flies up and down in the air. I can see that he is very much afraid of Anita.

It is dark when we arrive at my village of San Carlos. I had expected all my friends to be there waiting and cheering me, but instead there is not a soul in sight. Not even the town mongrel, Paco. We drive directly to my grandfather's hut. He comes to the door quickly when he sees the military car drive up.

"Abuelo! Abuelo!" I cry out. I hurry out of the car

and into his arms. So does Mama, who immediately starts to cry. Sometimes I wish she would grow up and behave like a strong woman, instead of like a little girl who is lost in the woods.

From Grandfather's arm I go into Grandma's, who is crying too. "My baby, my baby!" she weeps.

Anita stands talking to the Commandante near the hood of the car. I notice he gets into the car and drives away without so much as a goodbye. Well, I think, it doesn't matter. We are home safely and that's what counts.

"Anita, come over and meet my grandparents."

"Ah, yes. It is my pleasure to know the old ones in this family."

My grandfather nods and says, "Our home is yours. Thanks for bringing the children back home safely. For that we owe you much."

The old ones stay up late talking, laughing, and making plans. I am about to drift off to sleep when I hear a car screech to a rapid halt. Mama goes to the door and screams, then she bursts outside with such speed that I become alarmed. I get up to follow her, but Anita's hand holds me back.

"Wait, Kata. She's all right."

I turn to grandfather who smiles down at me. I have no choice but to wait until they consent for me to follow. The door opens and Mama enters beaming like a fresh morning sun.

"Papa!" I shout, as I run to embrace him. I leap like a frog into his open arms. "Papa's here! I told you he'd come back!"

"Yes, Kata. You did!" Mama puts her hand upon Papa's arm, caressing it gently.

"Let's wake Pablito!" I suggest.

"No," says Papa. "Let him sleep, for he can see

me tomorrow and many tomorrows after that. After all, I'm not going anywhere."

I frown and immediately set to scolding him. "Where have you been? We needed your help so much!"

He touches the tip of my nose. "I'm sorry, Kata. I know you needed me and I needed you. You see, I was in jail. That means locked up. When I was trying to make my way across the river, I turned in the wrong direction and landed back in Mexico. Since then I have been locked up in jail with no way out. Ah, I have been worried about the three of you and for many nights I cried and prayed to the good Lord for your safety."

He turns to Anita and says, "Señora, I owe you my entire life, as well as the lives of my family. If there is anything I can do, please let me know. The Commandante did not ask questions, but simply ordered my release and drove me out here himself. He is a true gentleman, no?"

"Certainly not, señor! He owes me a favor for his daughter's life," snaps Anita. "As for you, you should stop all that foolish dreaming and provide for your family. They have been through much pain and heartache, which will take many years to forget."

"You are right, señora."

"But," continues Anita in a soft voice, "it is good to hear thanks. Perhaps someday I will need a favor, which you will be so kind as to grant." She accepts his kiss on her palm.

"See, Anita!" I squeal, "I told you that you would like my Papa."

"Carlos," interrupts Mama. "Where did you get that stone Anita calls a nugget?"

"Nugget? A real gold nugget?!" Papa declares.

"Yes, it was," states Anita.

"I found that as I walked back from town. You see, I decided to take a short cut through the back hills. I grew tired and decided to sit near this large boulder. The stone was embedded in that boulder. I thought it looked different, so I dug it out with my knife and stuck it in my pocket."

Anita grunts, "Well, I sold it and got enough money to make you an important person around here. That is, if you use the money and your head properly."

"I was just going to clean it and make a pretty necklace for my wife," he adds as he runs his hand through her hair.

"Papa," I say, "Anita sold the stone for a lot of money. We could have a little ranchito like Anita's."

"If he uses his head, he could have many things," snaps Anita, as she crosses her arms over her breasts.

Papa starts to laugh and laugh until he hunches over in laughter. "But, señora. There are many more of those stones in that boulder. All I need to do is pick them!"

Anita's eyes blink rapidly. "My advice, señor, is to tell no one where that boulder is, or of the money you have here." Her chin begins to quiver and she stares straight at Papa.

He senses her seriousness. "It is wise advice, señora. My lips are sealed, but is it all right if I mail you a similar stone in payment for all you have done?"

"A postcard will do fine," smiles Anita.

"A postcard and a stone would be much better."

Anita throws her hand up into the air, "If you insist, señor."

"So be it, señora," smiles Papa, as he kisses Anita's palm again.

Anita's face glows, "Now I must take my leave with the Commandante. God bless you all."

"God go with you, Anita," I say, as I watch her get into the car.

"Anita, take care of yourself!" shouts Mama.

Anita turns back, then yells, "Make sure Kata goes to school. That is all that I ask!"

"I shall do that, Anita," smiles Mama as she continues to wave.

I break away from Papa and run into Anita's arm. "I shall miss you, old wise one."

"I shall miss you, Kata, my girl. May God be with you always."

"Always is such a long time, Anita," I answer laying my face upon her soft belly.

"And you are always welcome at my home, Kata."

"I love you Anita!" I shout as the car moves out slowly.

Across the Great River

by

Irene Beltrán Hernández

Across the Great River is an exciting tale of a young girl maturing and taking on the leadership role in her family when her parents become separated while illegally crossing the border into the United States. The family's experiences with labor smugglers, a folk healer and the authorities are told with the innocence and directness of a young girl who must face the harshness of life at an early age.

Across the Great River is recommended reading for young adult, as well as mature readers.

Irene Beltrán Hernández was raised in the Rio Grande Valley, the setting of her first novel, *Across the Great River*. She currently lives in Dallas.

ARTE PUBLICO PRESS
UNIVERSITY OF HOUSTON
HOUSTON, TX 77204-2090
713/749-4768

ISBN: 0-934770-96-4
LC: 89-289
PRICE: $8.50
TRADE PAPERBACK
YOUNG ADULT AND ABOVE
PUBLICATION DATE: JULY 15, 1989